MY FATHER AS AN ANT

&

OTHER STORIES

Also by Diana Hendry

POETRY

Making Blue (Peterloo Poets, 1995)
Borderers (Peterloo Poets, 2001)
Twelve Lilts: Psalms & Responses (Mariscat Press, 2003)
Sparks! with Tom Pow (Mariscat Press, 2005)
Late Love & Other Whodunnits (Peterloo Poets/Mariscat Press, 2008)
The Seed-Box Lantern: New & Selected Poems (Mariscat Press, 2013)
Second Wind with Douglas Dunn and Vicki Feaver (Saltire Society, 2015)

YOUNG ADULT NOVELS

Double Vision (Walker Books, 1990)
The Seeing (Corgi, 2012)

JUNIOR NOVELS

Harvey Angell (Julia MacRae/Walker Books 1991; Red Fox, 2003, 2012)
Harvey Angell & the Ghost Child (Julia MacRae/Red Fox, 1997, 2003, 2012)
Harvey Angell Beats Time (Red Fox, 2003, 2012)
Minders (Walker Books, 1998)
You Can't Kiss it Better (Red Fox, 2003)
Out of the Clouds (Hodder Children's Books, 2016)

PICTURE BOOKS

Christmas in Exeter Street (Julia MacRae, 1989)
The Very Noisy Night (Little Tiger Press, 1998)
The Very Busy Day (Little Tiger Press, 2001)
The Very Snowy Christmas (Little Tiger Press, 2005)
Oodles of Noodles (Little Tiger Press, 2008)
Dog Donovan (Walker Books, 1995)
Why Father Christmas Was Late for Hartlepool (Random House, 1995)

EDITOR WITH HAMISH WHYTE

Poems United (Scottish Poetry Library/Black & White Publishing, 2007)

EDITOR WITH GERRY CAMBRIDGE

The Rooftop Busker: New Writing Scotland 33 (ASLS, 2015)
Talking About Lobsters: New Writing Scotland 34 (ASLS, 2016)

My Father as an Ant

and Other Stories

◆

DIANA HENDRY

First published in the UK in 2017 by Postbox Press,
the literary fiction imprint of Red Squirrel Press
www.redsquirrelpress.com

Designed and typeset by Gerry Cambridge
www.gerrycambridge.com

A CIP catalogue record is available from the British Library.

ISBN: 978 1 910437 59 9

Cover image: © <ahref='https://www.123rf.com/profile_
yod67'>yod67 / 123RF Stock Photo</a>

Red Squirrel Press and Postbox Press are committed to
a sustainable future. This book is printed in the UK by
Ashford Colour Press using Forest Stewardship Council
certified paper.
www.ashfordps.co.uk

For Hamish, with love

CONTENTS

✦ My Father as an Ant ✦

WE KNEW MY FATHER WAS in the grip of another passion when he arrived home with a parcel almost larger than he could carry. There was that look on his face — part pride, part embarrassment — which signalled that a new, long-brooded dream had just hatched.

It was a well-padded parcel and with much huffing and puffing my father manoeuvred it down the hall and into the living room where he set it, triumphantly, on the sofa.

My father did his dreaming in the solitary confinement of his dressing room. Outside of it he was a remote man. Unknowable. And so large and lumbering, so heavy with weighty thoughts, that it was hard to imagine that any kind of passion or anything as light and airy as a dream could find an entry into such stolid flesh.

My mother did her best to warm him up, jollying him along, trying to teach him how to cuddle. Often she'd sit at the piano and play such tunes and songs you couldn't help but sing or dance to though he, locked in his armchair with the newspaper, did neither. Sometimes, to please her, he'd attempt a comic Charlie Chaplin waddle across the living room. But he never looked happy about it. Or comfortable. And because he was so big and awkward, what should have been funny was sad — like watching a circus animal perform.

My mother and sisters always said that I was his favourite. Indeed my mother would say, 'He didn't become a father until you were born'. The evidence for this was slight. I'd been known to sit on his knee. And some evenings I'd sit on the floor with my back against the arm of his chair and he'd take my nose between the knuckles of two fingers and tell me he was trying to lengthen it and make it like my mother's. I was proud of my snub and always worried that he might succeed, but I succumbed. He seemed to get some comfort from it. I was desperate to ask if it were possible, by continuous kneading and pulling, to lengthen the human nose, but I couldn't find anyone to ask and anyway, it was not an easy question to drop into a conversation. Nothing led up to it.

The parcel, when he'd removed layers of corrugated paper and old cloths, contained an oil painting. My mother was appalled. In her mind oil paintings belonged in museums or stately homes. And when she heard the price of it she rose to a pitch of moral indignation and calculated that the painting could feed as many people as Christ with the loaves and fishes. She reminded my father — as she always did when she thought he was getting above himself or about to be carried away by yet another expensive dream of grandeur — that in the great scheme of things he was only an ant. *An insignificant ant!*

I never could see my father as an ant, although I tried. He was such a big man and so uncomfortable in his body, that I thought that perhaps he might have liked being an ant, nimble and skittish on however many legs ants have, and indistinguishable from all other ants. But I couldn't shrink him. I could get as far as beetle or spider — because you can tell one beetle or spider from another — but not an ant. No, I saw him more as a stranded whale or walrus perhaps (he had a moustache) lumbering about our house and making the best of things but not exactly at home.

My mother tossed her head at the unwrapped canvas as if it was an insult to her house and slammed off into the kitchen. My father shufled his heavy feet, looked sheepish and hung the painting on the living room wall.

It was *The Swiss Alps at Sunset*. I was completely astounded. I'd never seen a mountain and suddenly here they were in our front room, cold, icy and wonderfully dangerous. My mother's moral disapproval made them almost illicitly exciting. And although a part of me knew that a painter had painted *The Alps at Sunset*, another part of me thought, irrationally, that these mountains had leapt straight out of my father's head onto the canvas.

I wondered if mountains were what my father had been dreaming about when, in the morning, he sat for hours in his dressing room smoking cigarette after cigarette. I speculated endlessly about what he was doing there. Sometimes I thought he was praying and that he had such a good rapport with God that he could carry on praying for hours. And sometimes I thought he had inside information about a second flood and was planning a new ark for us all. Or a quest that would involve great travel and adventure. My most recurrent fantasy was that he was like Jacob wrestling with the angel and saying, 'I will not let thee go except thou bless me', and that this was what kept him there, sitting in his old wicker chair, wrapped in his towelling dressing gown.

My mother said he was thinking about business and about his competitors, but unlike God and angels (pictured in my Bible book) 'business' was not something I could picture, let alone imagine thinking about for hours. The word 'competitors' perked me up a bit for I converted it to 'rivals' or 'enemies' and saw trench-coated gangsters from 'the flicks' with slouch hats and gun bulges in their pockets.

I knew that his dressing room and his office were the two places where my father dreamt his dreams. But then too, a mysterious aura of dream seemed to swirl around him like a big invisible hoola hoop from which, occasionally, a dream leapt out. A dream like the chandelier big enough for Cinderella's ball that now hung in our modest hall. ('Who d'you think you are? You're only an ant, an ant!') Or a dream like the billiards table — a big mahogany job, fit for a London Club and with a baize as smooth as a Wimbledon lawn — that now occupied what had been our dining room and was waiting, no doubt, for a group of aristocrats in evening dress to gather about it, chalking their cues, smoking cheroots, speeding the gleaming balls into the little rope nests at the four corners of the table or my father's universe.

But neither the chandeliers nor the billiards table gave me what *The Swiss Alps* and the paintings that followed the Alps, gave me. Windows into my father's hidden heart.

The second painting was quite different. It was small and dark but done up in a big, swirly gilt frame. It was called *The Monk and the Traveller* and because it was dark you had to peer at it very hard to see what was going on. I liked it because it seemed to tell part of a story and you could make up the rest of it yourself. The monk, plump and benign, and the traveller (who looked like a younger version of my father) sat at a rustic table. The monk had a glass of water and a cup of tea; the traveller a goblet of wine. The traveller had bare feet and wore sandals. He'd kept his knapsack on his back so he can't have been staying long. I thought perhaps the monk was advising him on his travels or pilgrimage and it confirmed my theory that my father was planning a quest.

I alternated between feeling deeply sorry for my large, lonely father and unbearably oppressed. Mornings were the worst. We'd be waiting, my mother and I, for the ant to finish wrestling with the angel, climbing the Alps, planning a quest or whatever and to descend from his dressing room dream. Waiting and waiting and waiting. My mother with the frying pan at the ready or the bacon drying hard in the oven and her ears, and mine, straining for the sound of his feet on the stairs.

They came down like doom. I'd be playing on the floor while he ate his breakfast, so I could see his legs and feet under the fringed cloth. I thought his heavy lace-ups might be half the trouble and that if he went about in bare feet and sandals (like the traveller in the painting) he wouldn't be so burdened. But even in his slippers he was heavy-footed.

When, at last, he'd finished his breakfast, had cleaned his plate of fried egg with a crust, had plodded down the long passageway that led to the garage, had sat warming the car's engine for at least five minutes, had — at last! at last! — eased the old Rover off and away into the purring distance, then the whole air of the house lightened with relief and my mother and I began our day.

Sometimes, since his death, I've wondered if my father had any character at all and if he used his hoola hoop of mystery to keep everyone from knowing this. Like Greta Garbo. Or perhaps he knew that if you keep quiet, other people invent a character for you, often making a more romantic job of it than any character you could create for yourself.

My mother got very huffy about the third painting which was loud and bright — as if my father had now thrown caution to the winds and was allowing himself to dream big. This time it wasn't the cost that offended my mother. It was the subject matter. *Spanish Women, Potting.* Even I, in my early teens by then, was alarmed to think that these great bosomy beauties had sprung — for I still thought of the paintings in this way — from my father's head. One woman wore a yellow rose in her hair. And it was not the pots that they shaped in their fine-fingered hands that drew the eye, but their low-cut dresses, their provocatively hitched-up skirts.

I'd thought my father was immune to women. I'd heard him say, of plain ones, 'All cats are grey in the dark'. And sometimes, chucking my mother under the chin, 'You're no oil painting, but you'll do.' Then I'd look at *Spanish Women, Potting* and wonder.

The last oil painting my father bought was called *Longing*. It showed a young boy trapped by the skein of wool he held for his mother while she grimly wound it into a ball. I remember the boy was all tightly bound up in his clothes although he had bare feet. He was hot with red-faced discomfort and wore his cap asquiff. You could tell he didn't want to be standing there, imprisoned by the loop of wool in his hands, because he looked longingly over his shoulder towards where the sun shone through an open door and where, I suppose, there were other children out in the true world, or dream world, of play.

By the time of the funeral my mother had long come to terms with *The Alps at Sunset*, *The Monk and the Traveller*, even *Spanish Women, Potting*. Although she never allowed herself to like any of them, she grew proud of them, recognising that the acquisition of paintings upped her status and gave the house that much sought-after commodity, class. And anyway, in his latter years my father was taken over by new passions — for pedigree dogs, ancient maps, fine port.

For many years I thought that that last painting, the one I think of as 'the boy prisoner', was the one that said most about what was in my father's heart. But nowadays I think I might have been nearer the mark when I imagined him, up in his dressing room, wrestling with an angel. And then it strikes me that this isn't true either, but has more to do with me, wrestling with the memory of my father. Still trying to know him.

◆ Trio ◆

ON THE TELEPHONE Ian is curt. Yes, he knows he promised to bring Alice home — Alice, moonlighting between mother and father — but there is this Very Important Conference and he is due to give a paper. Penny is quite prepared to take Alice half-way — to Birmingham, say — if she, Marie, will meet them there. He realises it may upset her plans, but this particular conference really is Very Important.

Oh yes, thinks Marie, the progress of science will be delayed at least half a century if Ian is not at the conference. But she is polite in that distant way one is with strangers, a politeness which has had to be re-acquired, slowly, in that long slow retreat from intimacy which is divorce.

That will be fine, she says. She will be quite happy to come as far as Birmingham to collect Alice. And where is the conference? Amsterdam? How nice. And how nice to meet Penny at last — this tossed off, lightly — maybe they can have a coffee together in the station buffet?

There is a short silence at Ian's end. He is remembering Marie, in a temper, hurling a champagne glass at the vicar's wife. Briefly he ponders the durability of British Rail crockery and is comforted.

Perhaps, perhaps, he says. But Penny is very short of time. Marie feels his alarm and rejoices. There is still a frisson in being able to disturb Ian.

When she puts the phone down she thinks, what shall I wear, and wonders why fashion editors are so limited in their notion of The Special Occasion — of which, Meeting-The-Other-Woman-For-The-First-Time, undoubtedly ranks high. Although now, which one of them, she or Penny, could claim the title 'The Other Woman'?

In a sudden vertigo she thinks that she and Penny might be one and the same person and a voice in her head says, as people say of sisters, or twins, 'You can hardly tell them apart'.

This is not quite true, Marie replies to the voice. What is truer is that Penny looks like I did twenty years ago. Yet it is a compliment, surely it is, to repeat, in the second wife, the looks of the first? Yes, yes — but the same can not be said of the other kind of repetitions. Alice, returning from her Christmas holiday, will bring back plenty of these. A bundle of them, like a bundle of old love letters.

Each repetition drops from her lips light and tinkling as a drawing pin but in Marie's mind takes on the reverberations of cymbals in an orchestra.

'Daddy is making wine,' Alice would say and in Marie's mind the memory rises of elderflowers or dandelions or chunks of parsnips; and then the demi-johns set on top of the dresser, breathing and bubbling through their tubes and eventually the syphoning into dark green bottles, the kitchen flags all wet, the neat knock of cork into bottle.

How beautiful it had been, this harvesting and distilling of the seasons and yet how it had weighed on her spirits, as if the whole process spoke of the years going on and on and on in a monotonous and endless cycle of elderflower, dandelion, parsnip; elderflower, dandelion, parsnip; so that it seemed an impossibility to get through all that wine or all those years — as indeed, maritally, it had been. Why was it that one bottle of darkly glowing elderberry should hold the essence of a timeless autumn but that bottles and bottles and bottles of the stuff should set up the drum beat, the foot-tramp of an awful infinity of years?

The more disturbing question is how can Ian begin all that again, from scratch, like a bankrupt? The tub, the demi-johns, the siphoning tubes, the bags of clean corks. It is wonderful human persistence. It is renewal. It is a terrible, terrible, unvarying perpetuity. For surely each repetition grew heavier than the one before? Second love carries first on its shoulders. Second loss bends the back lower than the first.

'Daddy is stacking logs,' Alice reports. 'He is making kitchen cupboards. At four o'clock he has a sandwich.' The small habits continued, babbling ever onwards like the brook, despite changes of women, seasons, addresses.

'They have pet names for each other,' says Alice. 'He's lion and she's squirrel, and when he's lion and she's squirrel they have a special talk that goes with it.'

And Marie winces. Not that she had been squirrel. What had it been? Mole and Badger? Petal and Flower? Ant and Bee? Did any of the names really matter? Were they not all interchangeable, all anonymous? There was simply a woman and a man and a repeated story, only when you were in it you had the illusion of being very intensely, very particularly, you.

Until now, Ian has kept Penny and Marie carefully apart. Penny exists for Marie as a voice on a telephone, a smile in a photograph, a tale told by Alice, a doppelganger, an understudy who has taken over, a squirrel evolving triumphant out of a Mole.

I shall wear a hat, thinks Marie and remembers the dark blue cloche that combines a look of intellectualism and jaunty dissipation. There is a script that goes with the dark blue cloche and the grey, elegant skirt, and another script for the green velvet hat and the jersey dress.

The blue hat and grey skirt for the demolition scene. The

skirt is narrow enough to allow her to 'draw herself up to her full height', for hauteur. The script is minimal. Either the melodramatic, 'See what you have done to my child!' (clutching Alice to her bosom, an undernourished version of Alice) or maybe simply a mime act, an expression of tragic contempt and her hand, moving out unexpectedly to deliver the classic 'stinging blow to the cheek'. That is the grey skirt and blue hat.

Now the red jersey dress — perhaps without hat? — for this is surely an indoor scene, set in front of a good fire, both of them on cushions, hugging their knees, firelight and brandy, cheeks aglow, laughing together, comparing notes on Ian's athlete's foot or sexual idiosyncrasies. It is possible, thinks Marie, that there is no closer kin than The Other Woman and no shared experience to match a shared man.

*

'You don't need to talk to her,' Ian says. 'You just deliver Alice and go.'

But it is not talking that worries me, Penny thinks, sitting on the train. It is seeing. Alice is reading. England goes by the windows as if someone has arranged for the view from train windows to stay forever constant.

Penny has a conversation on the brain, like a tune. It is her friend, Annette, hysterical over the ending of her affair with David. How the thing that had finished her off, just finished her off, was the way he would insist, whenever they played piano duets, on doing all the repeats, obeying every double dotted bar line, every 'from the beginning', 'da capo' instruction. How amusing Annette had been, describing how his tempo and her tempo were out of sync, she on bar 16, he on bar 20.

Perhaps, thinks Penny, I am at bar 16 and Ian at bar 20 in our lives. And then with a leap of thought, that she would have made a good wife for Bluebeard, that she would never have looked in the locked room where hung the corpses of past wives — never, never — and that she does not want to look now. She does not want to see Marie. It is, she thinks, infinitely worse meeting an alive ex-wife than seeing a dead one.

Of course when she and Ian had set up together, they had had it out about Marie. Now, as the cold clamped fields roll on (da capo, da capo, da capo) Penny wonders if she had only heard what she wanted to hear, if Ian had only told what he wanted to tell and if it was really only distance that had extinguished Marie in her mind. Until now, Ian's past, as represented by Marie, had been some 200 miles distant; another country.

Alice has fallen asleep. Her head lolls on Penny's shoulder. Alice, the image of Ian, they have always said. But she is not. See the chin, the long eyelashes ... she comes from the other country.

Penny looks at her reflection in the dark window. It perks her up. She is only 27. She is very attractive. She has a PhD. In the next year or two she and Ian will have a child. She has it all, youth, looks, the man and the work. Why then this terrible feeling of uncertainty, as though she were not quite herself but someone in a story?

She adjusts her hat — the blue cloche which makes her, she thinks, look like a Lawrence woman. But no, it is not that kind of story that she is in. Her story has been different, triumphant even. For had they not all — even Annette — shaken their heads and said 'He'll go back to his wife. You're wasting your time'. But he didn't and she hadn't. And Ian had come to her without a stick of furniture, without a stick of past — and happy about it, starting from the beginning, da capo.

Only, she thinks, there is no such thing. There can be no first time of anything for us. And suddenly she hates the landscape that represents the acres and acres of Ian that she will never know.

It has grown cold in the carriage. Will she, too, become Ian's past? Will he lock her up in the chamber of memory never to be visited? Without disturbing Alice, she wriggles her hand inside her bag to find her make-up. She will step elegantly off the train, composed, urbane. Alice will hold her hand. Marie will recognise, instantly, that she, Penny, is the better wife. Perhaps they will walk together down the platform, Alice between them — a hand each — and she will say, very quietly — conversationally — 'How could you do that to a man? How could you wreck him so?'

Or she would be evolved. Say how foolish it was in this day and age, not to be friends. Tea. Let us have tea. And over tea ask about Ian's youth, joke together about how he used to be and how he is now and then, then all that land, all those acres of Ian's past would be hers.

Alice stirs and stretches, looks surprised to find Penny beside her, says, 'Where are we?'

*

Ian is on the Amsterdam flight. Unbidden, a picture comes into his mind of his two women journeying from north and south — while he hovers over them in the air. He thinks of Donne's love poem to his wife when travelling to France, their two souls compared to 'stiffe twin compasses', one fixed at home while the other 'far doth rome' — and rejects it. The poem no longer works for him. Perhaps Penny and

Marie are now the 'twin compasses'. Perhaps he is just — ha! — the screw between them.

And anyway, there is Alice. It makes him sad to think of Alice whose childhood has become remarkably like his own. When he and Marie married he had sworn to himself that divorce was not something he would ever even consider. Nothing would allow him to put his own child through what he had been through. And then somehow it had all been repeated. Not the exact story of course, but a version of it.

He had not wanted them to meet, Penny and Marie, afraid, in the earlier days, of Marie's terrible temper. Yet, he thinks, opening up *The Times*, it wasn't simply Marie's temper that had made him go to such lengths to prevent a meeting. No, it was more as if some part of him which he didn't want revealed to either woman, would be revealed if both came together and that his whole being depended on not being wholly known, on keeping from both of them what both wanted: the silent heart of himself. Should either encroach on that private territory of self he could cut and run. Begin again. It was a pattern. His pattern. He could not escape it.

These are just the disorientated thoughts of flight, Ian decides, and he rustles the newspaper as if to shake the dust of time out of it. All these repeated stories. Page after page of them. And anyway, you could call it persistence, this ability — yet, it *was* an ability — to begin again. His scientific success is due entirely to that — the ability to try, try and try again.

He pictures Penny and Marie again, his 'stiffe twin compasses', talking and laughing together. Between them they are looking after him, maintaining the empty house of self while he is away.

The plane is coming in to land. Ian folds his paper, adjusts his face. He is a scientist going to a very important conference. He will deliver a splendid paper. The wives, past and present, will look after the empty house but neither of them will be able to get in. He has it well locked.

*

'There she is!' cries Alice. 'How funny! You're wearing the same hats!'

A very old drill of manners stirs in Marie's mind. She holds out her hand to Penny, says, 'Did you have a good journey?' At the same moment Penny too has put out her hand and is saying, 'I'm very pleased to meet you.'

*

Seeing her run towards him, Ian thinks, but of course, there is something about her that is like both of them.

She is laughing and kissing him. 'Tiger! Tiger!' she cries. Her laugh is like one of them, but which one? No, he is imagining things. She is different, new. A strange place, a strange woman. The relief of strangeness. It makes him feel on safe ground.

Conferences are like this. Everyone says so. It is the same old story. When he gets home it will be time to siphon the parsnip wine.

'My little bear!' he says tenderly.

◆ Coming Out ◆

INEVER WANTED TO GO north. I loved the phrase 'far north', but it existed only as a place in my imagination, a wild beyond, somewhere at the mind's extreme, somewhere one might go to howl at the moon and the gods and possibly die. I had as much intention of actually going there as I had of going to the Antarctic or the Sahara — places that also enjoyed a pleasing fantasy existence.

I was a small-town girl from the midlands. The holidays I'd been brought up to expect were southern seaside resorts in five star hotels overlooking a beach — preferably a posh beach with nothing more vulgar than a few worn-out donkeys and maybe a pier. Sometimes there was a theatre at the end of the pier offering amiable sub-standard family entertainment. But all that was before Lucas.

Until I met and married Lucas, four years ago, I don't think I'd been anywhere where there wasn't a bus stop in sight. And a shop. At least one shop. And a 'phone box. It occurs to me now that all three facilities offer the prospect of escape. The security of knowing you could escape. If you wanted to, that is. And because you could, you didn't usually want to.

But Lucas hankered for north. Lucas hankered for remote places. It didn't take me long, within the marriage, to realise that there was something remote in Lucas too. Mothers were the most important relationships in Lucas's life — his own and Mother Nature. It was Lucas's intention to introduce me to the latter and wean me from what he regarded, with scorn, as the bourgeois holidays of the nouveau riche.

He began gently enough with a holiday on the canals. I enjoyed this, the boat drifting quietly along passing places that clearly contained not only shops and 'phone boxes but pubs and people. Also we passed other canal boaters and could wave and smile at them. Sometimes we could even exchange a few words while struggling with the winding handle of a lock gate. But the most comforting feature of this holiday was that it would have been relatively easy to jump ship.

The second year I persuaded Lucas to holiday in France but made the mistake of letting him book it. It was a gite somewhere so deep in the Dordogne you might have sunk without trace if you'd stayed there longer than a fortnight. Either it wasn't isolated enough for Lucas or it wasn't his kind of Remote because he was gloomy for the entire two weeks. Only Scottish Remote, it seemed, kept Lucas happy. So the next year I agreed to a holiday in Caithness.

The cottage we rented must have been some kind of hunting lodge. It was full of diaries recording what had been killed and when. There was a deer's head, or something like it, fixed on the wall and a marble slab outside the back door for cutting up fish, fowl, monsters. It was depressing in the extreme. The landscape of bare rocks and stones looked to me like some part of the world left over after the Creation. Either that, or God's reserve stock of building bricks should He wish to start again from scratch.

I think even Lucas must have realised he was pushing his luck for this year he suggested a holiday on Skye. He had his thesis to finish. He needed solitude, concentration, space. We could, he said, rent a croft house on Skye for a month. I liked the word 'croft', imagining a stone built, thatched cottage. Maybe a vegetable garden, maybe neighbouring crofts. I'd heard about ceilidhs, weaving, the beauty of the Cuillins.

The croft turned out to be a big grassy nowhere with a newly built bungalow in the middle of it. You came off the road and drove down a long, rough track. In the distance I could see two or three other crofts, their houses crouched apologetically on the landscape, their roofs held down by stones as if they feared being ripped from their roots by a wind with the force of the wrath of God. The road at the end of the track led in one direction, some three miles away, to the only shop. A shed, more than a shop, selling white sliced bread, turnips and twenty-five varieties of whisky. Seven miles away, in the other direction was a distillery which was as far as the milkman was prepared to come to deliver milk.

Without buildings around me I felt strangely unprotected. And then I hardly knew the name of anything. The land round our croft, for instance, was neither field, garden nor meadow. It gave me an odd kind of claustrophobia, all that space and nowhere — I mean nowhere *particular* to go.

The house itself contained the largest deep freeze I have ever seen and a quantity of tacky ornaments that we put away on arrival. On the far side of the track there was a washing line. I enjoyed the washing line, pinning clothes out in what felt like not just the wind of Skye, but the wind of the world. Under the big blowy sky of Skye the clothes looked like dolls' clothes.

Lucas had never been happier. In the morning he worked on his thesis. In the afternoons he went walking, alone, so he could think about it while collecting the milk. He was so at home that he seemed to grow and stretch. I watched his back lose its hunch, his legs stop their nervous twitching. Me? I felt I was growing smaller and smaller, shrinking into insignificance like the dolls' clothes on the line. Nor was it just the space and the silence that shrank me like an Alice in Strange-land until I began to doubt my own existence. It was the lack of people.

At the road end of the track there was a shed occupied by Mr McLeod and his loom. A wooden sign, pointed to the shed and tacked on a post, said 'Weaving'. On the three occasions that I visited Mr McLeod the loom remained resolutely still and Mr McLeod as resolutely silent. Maybe he had set himself up as a tourist attraction and had lost heart waiting for orders that never came. Or else he was in hiding from some harridan of a wife. At any rate I gave up any attempt at a conversation as I did in the shop where the locals reverted to talking in Gaelic as soon as I appeared.

That left the boy. A wild-haired boy who appeared one afternoon in our second week, riding down the track on his bicycle and coming right up to the house. I reasoned he was the son of the crofter and resented his home being rented out to tourists because he refused a cup of tea and told me he had come to tell me he'd seen the Death Cart on the road.

'The Death Cart?'

'It's black,' he said. 'You only see it when someone's about to die'. And away he rode.

I was charmed and amused. I told Lucas about him. Said how nice it was that there were children who still believed in folklore or legend, thinking that the Death Cart presumably belonged to one or the other.

Of course I'd anticipated spending a lot of time on my own. I'd brought my sketch pads, charcoal, watercolours, a stack of novels. I hadn't lived with Lucas for four years without knowing that I'd need resources. But I couldn't begin on anything. I sat on the back doorstep looking down the track and daydreamed a brass band coming down the distant road bringing life, vitality, music.

I suppose I must have reached some kind of pitch of claustrophobia and it was this that drove me out one afternoon to walk. To walk despite the grey gloom of the day. To walk without thinking of going anywhere — an idea quite alien to my small town self. Behind the croft was moor and peat bog. I'd learnt the names now. I wrapped up warm and set off. Almost at once, my mother's voice, coming from childhood, began its customary warning — *Don't go off the beaten track! Don't go off the beaten track!* Mother, I wanted to say, no-one could be more off the beaten track than I am at the moment and I felt quite pleased with myself. Childishly defiant.

Things might have turned out differently if it hadn't been for the man who suddenly loomed out of the moor, bent double under a large black sack. By then I'd been walking for about two hours. I'd been thinking about Lucas. Thinking that some people relate more to animals than humans and that others, like Lucas, relate more to landscape than people. I was wondering if my apparent need of buildings implied that I should become an architect. I fantasised about what I might build and then reasoned I'd probably get little choice. By then, by the time the man appeared, the light had changed. Rather there was less of it as dark clouds bunched themselves up and a kind of light, shivery wind ran through the thin moor grass.

The man's figure was the incarnation of whatever danger lurked *off the beaten track*. Whatever or whoever. It was as if my mother's voice from the grave was saying, *I told you so!* My first thought was that the bulging sack under which the man stooped, contained a body he was about to bury. Any man wandering the moor alone and with sack, could not be anything else but a murderer. Probably a serial one for as witness to his crime I would surely be next. Here was the bogey man of bogey men. And had I not been warned, twice warned, by my mother and the boy? The boy who I now believed had second-sight. He'd seen the Death Cart. And at that moment, so did I.

I was far away from the croft. Far away from the road. There was no-one in sight. The moor itself, full of lumps and swampy ditches was not easy to run across and besides, the man had only to drop his sack and he'd be upon me. Even if I shouted, no-one would hear. It flashed across my mind that my murdered body would be almost impossible to find and I pictured Lucas striding across the moor looking for me and — in a way — enjoying himself as he trampled heedlessly over my buried remains.

Having decided that my end was near, a strange kind of calmness came over me, almost as if this was quite an appopriate way to die, under this big sky, on this empty stretch of moor. It had a certain almost majestic destiny about it.

It was only when the man was a few feet away that I realised what his sack contained. The weight that had bent him double was peat. And now that I looked, really looked, I saw that there were peat diggings, peat stacks like primitive grave diggings, all over the moor. From under his sack the man nodded at me, gave a grunt that might have been a Gaelic good afternoon, and vanished into the gloom.

A curious lightness came upon me as if I'd suddenly been released. As if, from now on, I was free to go off the beaten track whenever and however I liked. Alone. It was as if I'd come out into the world for the first time. And yes, I was small, very small and insignificant — so insignificant that I had no other choice than to begin to be myself. So I carried on walking. Walking and walking and walking until I reached the road and even then I kept on walking.

I left the island of course. And I left Lucas. And when I got back to the mainland it felt as if the choice was simple. I headed north. Far north.

◆ Between Foolishness and Wickedness ◆

'THEY WERE GOING TO DROWN you when you were born,' says Hetty's Grandad. 'Like they drown kittens down a well.'

Hetty ignores him. Grandad is always saying things. Oh, the things he says! Hetty's mother says you can't take Grandad anywhere because of the things he says. Take him to a decent restaurant and what does he do? Acts common. Calls the waitress 'love' and pinches her bottom. He's a silly old man, that's what Hetty's mother says.

So this about drowning kittens — well, Grandad has said it before and will probably say it again. It washes over Hetty's head as she sits on the floor with an array of dolls, semi-absorbed in some story of her own. Overall, Hetty does not mind Grandad's silliness. Indeed she is rather fond of it — and of him. Foolishness in a grown-up is something of a relief if you are surrounded, as Hetty is, by grown-ups who, by their every move and gesture indicate omnipotence.

Grandad does not. Every Saturday morning he trots down the hill from his small house to Hetty's big house, a clown-like figure in one of his son's hand-me-down (or is it up?) suits. The shoulder-pads of the jacket, extending beyond Grandad's own shoulders, curl at the corners like budding wings. The trousers bloom at his hips and concertina at his ankles. When he arrives, the remaining quiff of his white hair has been blown into a little cockatoo, his face is pink as a stick of rock and he is glad to sit down.

He sits in the reproduction Jacobean carver that is padded with leather and studded round the back and the seat so that it is not unlike a throne — though a throne of a rather plain variety, Protestant perhaps, rather than Catholic. But this is appropriate for Grandad who is not, after all, very grand.

So Grandad sits in his plain Protestant throne and Hetty, his acolyte — prone to bouts of silliness herself from time to time — attends to his needs, which are a bottle of beer, a pipe of St Bruno tobacco and homage. They are a pair, Hetty and her Grandad. For two hours every Saturday morning, Hetty is a Somebody and Grandad is a Somebody.

'They wanted a boy,' Grandad says, pursuing his story while Hetty pursues hers with the dolls. 'They didn't want another girl. If you'd have been a boy, they'd have called you David.'

Sometimes Hetty allows this piece of silliness a place in her mind. There is a boy at school called David. He is blonde and sturdy and smiling. I would have been like him, Hetty thinks, and if she could volunteer to start again and this time come on stage as a blonde and smiling David, then she would do. Anything to oblige.

Hetty likes looking after Grandad on a Saturday morning. He shows her how to open the bottle of beer — easing the frilly little metal cap off with the opener — and then pouring the beer, very, very slowly and steadily into the glass, holding the glass at just the right angle so that the beer flows clear right to the top of the glass when it is allowed its delicate trim of froth. If you do it wrong, the froth comes too soon, the beer is cloudy and the contents of the bottle won't fit the glass. It is a highly skilled occupation and Grandad is a stern judge of its performance. Hetty likes doing this for Grandad and Grandad likes Hetty doing it for him, sitting on his throne, lord and vassal, saving your grace.

When the beer is poured, Hetty sits back on her heels

and watches while Grandad fills his pipe. The old brown pipe, his yellow plastic pouch of tobacco and his box of Swan Vesta are brought ceremoniously forth from his baggy pocket.

The wood of the pipe has the gloss of use. The bowl is burnt black as a fire grate. Hetty watches as Grandad takes the golden brown tobacco from the pouch and rubs it through his thumb and forefinger until it is shredded to his satisfaction. Then it is packed down into the bowl, thumbed in, and at last, clenching the pipe's stem in his mouth, Grandad applies several matches to the gold stuff. He holds each match so long that Hetty holds her breath in case he burns his fingers. The burnt bodies of the matchsticks are tossed aside, the strange little haystack inside the bowl kindles, and eureka! The pipe is going! Grandad cups the warm bowl in his hand, draws in and exhales the sweet and saintly Bruno. Later he will scrape out the dead ashes with one of the burnt matchsticks, knock them into the ash-tray and then pipe, pouch and matches go back in his pocket. Saturday morning's eucharist is over.

During this time, Hetty's father is at work. Hetty's sisters, much older and recovering from Friday night dances and dates, are asleep. Hetty's mother is in self-chosen exile in the kitchen.

From ten to twelve on a Saturday morning, Hetty and Grandad have the world and the breakfast room to themselves. Grandad isn't grand enough to be entertained in the lounge where the objects which certify his son's post-war prosperity have accumulated — an ebony grand piano, an oil painting, an ornate chandelier.

But the breakfast room is not without grandeur. There are brass candlesticks on the sideboard, velvet curtains, a fringed maroon undercloth on the table. There is Grandad's throne and there is the sunlight which, in the morning (and maybe on a Saturday morning in particular), comes through the breakfast room windows and makes a misshapen rug of itself on the floor where Hetty sits and makes up stories with her dolls while Grandad, on high, makes up stories about drowning kittens and little boys named David.

Hetty's mother keeps in the kitchen as long as she can because of honouring thy father and mother (which includes your husband's). She cannot manage much of this. Indeed, almost none. 'He's never done a decent day's work in his life,' Mrs Worthing tells Hetty as often as Grandad tells her about the kittens. 'He spends every night in the pub. If it wasn't for your father, he'd be in a Salvation Army hostel by now.'

Hetty, imagining the Salvation Army to be a breed of angels assigned to the task of providing accommodation in heaven, takes this to mean that without her father's care, Grandad would be dead.

'Your father buys him a house,' continues Mrs Worthing, 'And gives him money ... *and* suits ....'

'They're too big,' says Hetty.

'And every Christmas,' Mrs Worthing sweeps on, 'he comes to stay and every Christmas he gets tiddly.'

Mrs Worthing never uses the word 'drunk'. It is common. Also 'tiddly' is more appropriate to a silly old man.

In this way Hetty is made aware of the gulf between her father and her grandfather. Her father works all the hours God gives and is never tiddly. Furthermore, by his heroic efforts (for which they should all be grateful) he has built himself a business and this has allowed them to receive the rewards which God gives to the virtuous. Oil paintings, chandeliers, velvet curtains. The suits he passes on to his father are of the finest cloth and tailor made. It is the old man's foolish fault if he is not big enough, in body or spirit, to fit them.

All by his very own efforts, Mr Worthing has made himself as grand as the ebony grand piano, as grand as velvet; grand, much grander than grandfather. She should remember, Mrs Worthing tells her daughter, that during the war — that war in which children just like Hetty, (only wearing armbands with a star on them) had been sent to their deaths in gas chambers — during that war, Hetty's father, her own dear father, had been a firefighter in the city. He had stood aloft on the towers of the town and kept Hitler at bay, had kept guard over them all, like God. Even Grandad, tiddly in the pub no doubt, and Grandma too, sad and penny pinching at home and dead now, poor dear, much afflicted by the silliness of Grandad as she was.

This knowledge makes it difficult for Mrs Worthing to honour thy father-in-law as she should and so she keeps to the kitchen, afraid she will not be able to hold her tongue and that one day, as she warns Hetty, she will come right out with it and say, 'You are a very silly old man.'

Mr Worthing goes to work on a Saturday morning because work is much better than staying at home and because he has a new Rover and likes to drive it into town on a Saturday morning and because if he is back by noon there will be time for a half-hour chat with the old man and half an hour is quite enough, thank you. Mr Worthing has a motto. 'Be nice to the people you meet on the way up; you might meet them on the way down.' This includes his father.

Mrs Worthing, having studied respectability and the mores of the middle class from all angles, has no intention of ever going down. Nor have her elder daughters whose boyfriends are regularly and lewdly (in their opinion) questioned by Grandad about their intentions.

Mrs Worthing and the girls recall the important wedding of a business acquaintance to which they had been foolish enough to take Grandad. They recount the way he stole cigars and how, more than tiddly, he toppled down a flight of stairs and instead of lying decently dead at the bottom of them, indecently bounced upright again, pinker than before, but with neither his quiff nor his spirits quelled.

It is a tale they tell and re-tell, groaning and laughing at the embarrassment of it all. Hetty, thinking of the way clowns win applause by tumbling downstairs and falling over themselves, has difficulty understanding this story.

Mr Worthing does not waste his energies on feelings of shame and embarrassment. The old man is the old man. Besides, he has bought him. The house, the quarterly allowance, the good suits, these favours keep the old man quiet. They buy peace and quiet. Money talks, thinks Mr Worthing and in this instance it buys silence. He is pleased with this paradox. He will be home by twelve. Half an hour of the old man will be quite enough. Women and girls are better company for an old man.

For Hetty, the culmination of the morning's ritual is the Saturday sixpence. It has to be won. First by homage and tribute, and then physically won, for Grandad puts the sixpence inside his clenched fist and Hetty has to unbend his fierce old fingers to reach it. Often she unlocks two fingers only for them to clamp back down again as she forces up a third. Sometimes, to distract her, Grandad lets his upper dentures drop and clack and Hetty, in a fright, lets go of his hand altogether. The sixpence becomes more and more precious.

As soon as she has it, Hetty is released from service. She runs to the newsagent's to buy a notebook. It is always a notebook. Hetty collects them. She doesn't write in them. She likes the possibility each blank sheet presents of a new start, of re-writing a life in which kittens aren't drowned and children with stars on their arms are carried straight to the kingdom of heaven where the salvation army of angels are waiting and where Grandad's shoulder pads have at last flowered into wings.

ii

'It's ridiculous at his age,' says Mrs Worthing. 'You tell him. Tell him he's ridiculous.'

'He's my father,' says Mr Worthing who has every intention of doing just this. He gives his wife a look of great virtue. Behind his tortoiseshell framed spectacles, bought for their appearance of business gravitas, Hugh Worthing has very pale blue eyes. It is hard to tell whether all dark thoughts have been washed out of his eyes or if there was nothing there in the first place.

Because of the formal interview to come, the Worthings are in the lounge. From his own armchair Mr Worthing has a view of the entire room while remaining closest to the fire. Two Saturday newspapers are laid on the table beside him. The ebony piano glows briefly in the corner of his eye. Mrs Worthing fusses about him, wafting to and fro like a human fan.

However, even though Mr Worthing is lord of all he surveys with his pale blue, innocently ruthless eyes, he can not see through sofas and is therefore unaware — as is

Mrs Worthing — of his youngest daughter, Hetty, hiding behind it.

The position of the sofa provides Hetty with a strange view of the room. The angle between the wall and the sofa forms a slit window which, if it were higher, might be suitable for arrows. To observe the room, Hetty has to twist her head 90 degrees to the right.

What she sees, at the moment, is her father safe and solid in his chair and by this fact she knows that all is well with the world. Or reasonably well, because Hetty also sees her mother pacing up and down and knows that she is both angry and anxious. And because this Saturday morning is different from all other Saturday mornings, she knows that something is up. Enigmatic comments during the preceding week suggest that Grandad, in his silliness, has surpassed himself.

Hetty knows that there is a thin line of difference between mere silliness which, at school, might make Miss Clingoe summon you to her room for a telling-off, and downright wickedness for which, last term, Annabel Minto, was expelled. By her mother's grim face, the pursed mouth of the righteous, Hetty knows that Grandad has mysteriously crossed this border between foolishness and wickedness, so she hides behind the sofa, half excited, half afraid, but trusting — trusting that her father, a figure hewn out of solid English oak as he sits now in the big chair of justice, will heroically rescue Grandad and that Grandad, although he may topple down innumerable flights of stairs, will always bounce upright again. Irresponsible, irrepressible, silly.

'You're too good to him,' Mrs Worthing coos at Mr Worthing. 'A house, an allowance, your best suits long before they're worn out ..... What more does he want? Send him off with a flea in his ear!'

Mr Worthing, aware that he is being stiffened for battle, and having a fine command of Churchillian epigrams left over from the war, pats his wife's bottom as she passes and quotes, 'It was the nation and the race that had the lion's heart. I had the luck to be called upon to give the roar.'

Mrs Worthing is cheered. 'That's right!' she says, soothing his mane. 'You roar!'

Hetty is cheered too. Clearly Grandad is to be defended. The lion will roar. Grandad's enemies will scatter.

'Roar and scare his pants off!' Mrs Worthing urges.

'My pants,' says Mr Worthing. 'And in the circumstances, we want him to keep them on.'

'He's seventy-seven,' says Mrs Worthing. 'It's disgusting at his age.'

'I suppose he's been lonely since Ma died.'

'He's got his pals at the Beaufort Arms.'

'Not quite the same, is it?'

'You haven't seen her, Hugh! A dyed blonde. Sixty if she's a day and dyed blonde. Rattling with cheap jewels. All from Woolworth's. I know her sort. She wants to take him for a ride. Wants to take us for a ride!'

(In her time, Mrs Worthing has also rattled with cheap jewels, but now that she has acquired more respectable habits, any form of vulgarity offends her the way cigarette smoke offends one who has given up tobacco).

Hetty tries to adjust her head and her thoughts. She cannot work out who is the enemy, who is to be roared at. She thinks there are two contenders: the man with pants that need scaring off and the dyed blonde.

'Of course she's got nothing,' says Mrs Worthing. 'Fancies she'll inherit the house — our house — and the allowance — our money — no doubt. I tell you Hugh, that woman's a blood-sucking bat.'

Hetty tries to turn the dyed blonde into a bat but the blondeness makes such a metamorphosis difficult.

'Oh he's cunning, all right,' says Mrs Worthing. 'Plays on your generosity. Expects you to carry him on your back.'

Hetty abandons the dyed blonde and returns to the man-with-pants-that-need-scaring off.

'We shall defend our island,' says Mr Worthing looking about him with his pale eyes, as if the chandelier, the fitted carpet, the new rustic brick fireplace, are under threat of falling down. 'Victory at all costs,' he says.

'Victory at no *extra* cost,' says Mrs Worthing.

'What time is he coming?'

'Eleven, he said.'

'You keep out of it. Leave it to me,' says Mr Worthing. Happily Mrs Worthing departs for the kitchen, leaving the deed to him. Mr Worthing takes up his newspaper.

Hetty is quite snug behind the sofa. She has brought her pillow, her best doll and her security blanket. She is half inclined to sleep a little while waiting for Grandad. Being behind the sofa, hidden like this, makes her feel funny. As if she is here and yet not here. She thinks about crawling out and saying 'Boo'. But she is cross. Saturday morning is her morning, the morning she and Grandad are Somebodies. Then she feels guilty because after all, Grandad needs defending by the lion and she ought not to mind. But today there will be no sixpence and no magic with the beer and the pipe and it is a very long time until next Saturday.

When she wakes up it is too late to come out and say 'Boo'. Grandad is already there. She is stuck behind the sofa and dare not come out. From being a powerful spy she is now a prisoner.

It is the tone of the voices that imprisons her, and the change in the light. Between her sleep and her wakening the weather has changed. The distorted vision provided by Hetty's arrow window is darkened. There is a sharp draught from the door Mrs Worthing has left open, probably so that she can eavesdrop.

The man in the big chair of judgement has changed. The oak of England seems to have taken root. There is something immovably solid about him so that Hetty feels that if she were to reach out to him he would not be able to respond. And surely his feet have grown to an enormous crushing size? The shine on his toe-caps is as bright as knives. Hetty can see that his face is turned towards the old man but she cannot see the eyes behind the spectacles. He has no eyes. There are just blank circles of glass where eyes should be.

Because of the darkening weather, Mr Worthing switches on the light. It catches the lens of his spectacles and flashes off Grandad's watch. Or maybe the beam goes in the opposite direction, so that it is the flash from Grandad's watch that has burnt out the eyes behind the spectacles. Hetty is uncertain.

Grandad, in his smaller chair, is not the Grandad of other Saturday mornings. His little budding wings look more like horns. The clown has died in his face. He is all knobs and angles and has turned a strange colour. Hetty sees how the veins in his hands have come to the skin's surface and wriggle there like fat worms. Seeing his hands Hetty remembers the fierceness of his grip when she tries to prise the sixpence from his palm. Hetty has never thought her Grandad ugly until now. For some reason she thinks of the little boy David she should have been. As David, she would not now be crouched unseen, unheard, behind the sofa. She would be a somebody; a blonde, sturdy and smiling somebody and there would be three of them — grandfather, father, son.

Both men are very angry. Someone has come along and screwed up their faces as if they were made of plasticine.

'All goodness and light, aren't you?' sneers the old man. 'Look at you, all got up grand in your grand house with your grand family. Well I know you .... I know what you are. And don't you forget it!'

There is something about the old man's anger, his redness of face, his shaking fingers, the tick in his cheek that makes Hetty want to cry.

Mr Worthing is so still that Hetty thinks he has turned to stone. He has no eyes and has turned to a block of stone. When he drums his fingers on the arms of his chair, she is relieved that he can still move.

He says, 'I think of my mother ....'

'Your mother!' screeches the old man. 'Did you think of her when she was alive eh? Eh? You great hypocrite you! When did you visit? Never! That's when. Always us coming to see you. The beggars visiting the rich man in his castle. The rich being all magnanimous. I've heard you murmuring in boardrooms about looking after your old Dad. Murmuring and modest. Boasting! Sick boasting! Us always having to visit you. Me crawling down the hill every Saturday. You giving me half an hour of your precious time.'

'No-one asks you to visit,' says Mr Worthing.

'Oh no! No-one asks me!' says the old man, bitterness calming him down. 'Who are you really looking after, Hugh? Me or your dirty conscience?'

Mr Worthing stands up. For a moment, as he leans against the side of the fireplace nearest to her arrow window, Hetty sees the full giant size of him. She has been peering out from such an odd angle and for so long that she begins to feel dizzy.

'What's my conscience to you?' asks Mr Worthing advancing on his father. 'You just take, take, take as though I owed you. What do I owe you? Sweet bloody nothing! Where I've got today is not because of you. It's in spite of you. But always you make out I owe you. Well, get this into your dumb old head. I may owe you for being born but I don't owe anything to some blonde old cow that you want to set up with. Marriage! At your age! Don't make me laugh. What she wants is to marry my — yes, my house — and my money. That's what she wants. Thinks it won't be long before you're dead and buried and then watch her! I doubt she'll bother to wrap you in your shroud before she's off to the bank, staking her claim.'

The old man gets to his feet. He is very unsteady. He wobbles like he does when he is tiddly. Hetty sees that he has something dark in his hand and for a moment thinks it is a knife. He is going to stab her father. But no! It is only his old pipe.

Mr Worthing hasn't finished. He is shouting loudly now. Roaring like a lion and the noise is right inside Hetty's head. It is so loud she can't hear the words, only the roar. She covers her ears with her hands and then she can hear better.

'Go ahead with this and that's the last you'll hear from me!' shouts Mr Worthing. 'Understand? Not another penny. And don't think you can come creeping round here on a

Saturday morning, sucking up to Martha, trying to win the kids. They all know what an old sot you are. What a leech.'

Grandad is still clutching his pipe. Hetty sees that he has trouble with his false teeth. It happens sometimes when he stands up too quickly. Probably they have worked loose from making too many ghoulish faces at Hetty on a Saturday morning. The old man's hands are shaking too much for him to push the teeth back in. He has gone very pale. His head is like a skeleton's. Hetty sees that his eyes are the same colour as her father's and wonders that she has never noticed this before.

The old man is exactly lined up with her arrow window now. Hetty sees nothing comic or silly about Grandad, only his pale eyes and his face twisted in anger and his teeth dropping.

Hetty feels dizzier and dizzier. The space behind the sofa has become unbearably claustrophobic. It is a terrible place and she doesn't know how to get out. She is trapped here and the sofa is tipping slowly backwards as in a nightmare and she hasn't the strength to ward it off, to hold it up. The weight of the huge sofa will crush and suffocate her. But it is not the sofa falling. It is Grandad. Very slowly he falls, with his mouth wide open so that the false teeth drop and bounce on the floor and the roaring that has been in Hetty's head becomes Grandad's strange, strangled, almost child-like cry.

✦ The Novel Novel Paper ✦

i

THEY HAVE GIVEN US forty-eight hours. Forty-eight hours and three questions. It is like something out of a fairy-tale. It is like being shut in the king's palace and told to spin straw into gold or to guess Rumpelstiltskin's name. Answer three questions and your reward shall be a degree in your pocket. Fairy gold.

All the other Finals papers have been the standard three hour affairs — the Big Hall, the boom of Big George, gruesome lucky mascots blossoming out of inkwells, one hundred and twenty minutes in which to tell (selectively) all you have learnt in three years about Shakespeare, or American Lit., or the romantic poets. An unfair absurdity, but a known, familiar, dear absurdity.

So then someone in the English Department, someone of fair and creative mind, thinks this one up — the forty-eight hour Novel Paper. You can imagine them, the dozen fey souls of the English Department, at five o'clock on a Friday, waxing creative over a bottle of sherry. It was probably Leonie Pipforth, new last year, the bearer of the awful tidings of literary theory, she who did an entire PhD on *The Use and Abuse of Parenthesis by Poets* and who tutors on the 19th century novel with her 20th century boots up on the table. Or it could have been Prof. Larch, about to be brain-drained to America and practising innovation. Or Dr Loupher in a bored and drunken moment.

'All the students have to do is to remember the plots of three novels, mug up some old essays and a few quotes and they're through,' says Pipforth/Larch/Loupher. 'The exam should be a test of intelligence, not memory. Students should have their books about them. They should have time. Being English students they should be able to write!' Such moral earnestness could not have been gainsaid. (Archaic or literary word. I am bringing it back into common usage. What use is knowledge unless it is applied?) Collectively, the English Department would have nodded their story-filled heads and gone off home feeling expansively experimental.

And this is why I am here, at this station of the cross, the Handing Out of the Novel Paper, with my companions of three years, Jane, Peter, Alice and Sebastian. It is 9.30 a.m. on Monday, 21st of May. (An actual date gives a piece of fiction authenticity. You will be more inclined to believe the rest of this, even if I am making it up, which I might or might not be).

We may take the exam paper whither we wish. (My prose is understandably nervy). Jane goes to her flat. Sebastian goes to the library. Alice goes the Lord-knows-where. Possibly to drown herself considering the quantity of notes she has made on *Middlemarch*. Peter goes to wait for the pubs to open. I, being of so-called mature years (thirty-nine plus seven months and twenty two days) take my paper home, hoping I will not crash the car on the way, thereby obliterating all of the forty-eight hours.

What, in the name of Proust, made them come up with the figure of forty-eight? It is an unliterary span of time if ever there was one. Literature cannot thrive without the figure three. Three sons, three fates, three wishes, three Unities, Act Three of every Shakespeare play.

On the third day, Christ rose. He could not have done so on the second day. All the drama of the Passion would have been lost.

So what was wrong with thirty-six hours or three days for the novel paper?

ii

I would be better off locked in a chamber of the palace with a load of straw than shut in my own front room with three centuries of the English novel on the shelf before me. I have to spin them into three essays totalling four thousand words.

In a palace, with straw, I could be outside time. The world would go on without me. Here, adrift in fictional time, physical time flurries about me. The gas-man cometh to read the meter. The vicar calls for coffee. A friend with a marital crisis that belongs in a Margaret Drabble novel telephones her troubles. All three think my statement that I am sitting a forty-eight hour Novel Paper is an unlikely story. This makes me think that it is a very likely story. A radio play perhaps. Or more profitably, television. Forty-eight hours in the lives of Jane, Alice, Peter and Sebastian, each character linked to a fictional one — Jane/Emma, Alice/Tess, Peter/Tristram, Sebastian/Sebastian.

I think about writing this instead of answering the questions on the Novel Paper. At thirty-nine years, seven months and twenty-one days, do I need a degree? I did not come to University with expectation of any kind. Of Love or of Bright Shining Futures. (I have a fondness for the capital letter as used in the late 18th century).

I came, creature of the twentieth century as I am, as to a convalescent home. Me with my broken down nerves, disconnected, alienated, confused, post-divorce, post almost everything modern, having known, like Beckett's Ruby Tough, 'an almost atomic despair'. (Oh I can shake a phrase if not a leg. 'Do not use "oh" lightly' my tutor says. 'An "Oh!" must be rare and earned.') I came not knowing if Jane Austen came before Laurence Sterne or Wyatt before Donne or death before life.

And here I have been healed. Reconnected. I have lamented with 'The Wanderer' and 'The Seafarer'. They have lulled the spirits of my not so vasty deeps with the medieval lyric, rocked me in the cradle of the epic, soothed all my metaphysical feathers and given unto me Wordsworth's *Prelude*. Yes, yes, I know there is a worrying lack of sex in *The Prelude* but I refound my childhood there and was given permission, licence to imagine things. Let the cliffs arise and stride after me. All shall be well, and all manner of things shall be well.

(Oh!) my alma mater, forgive me if I jest about the Novel Paper and trespass in the house of fiction.

iii

When the gas-man and the vicar have gone, I read the examination questions. They are divided into two parts. I am to choose two questions (out of sixteen) from Section A and one question (out of eight) from Section B. In Section B, some wit has chosen the final paragraphs of eight major works. I am to comment on the substance and the style.

'A Cock and a Bull, said Yorick — And one of the best of its kind, I ever heard.' (*Tristram Shandy*).

'Yes, she thought, laying down her brush in extreme fatigue, I have had my vision.' (*To the Lighthouse*).

'..... his heart was going like mad and yes I said yes I will Yes.'(*Ulysses*).

I sat, in the testing early hours of the forty-eight, before the three centuries of English (and Irish) fiction on the shelf and thought about endings. The ending of youth, of love, of dreams, of life. The finality of finals. And I thought about not beginning at all. I lay down on the sofa for a long time and thought about that final 'Yes' of *Ulysses* and how fitting it was and how there is no other word worthier of being the last one of a novel or of a life. One should face death not with an 'Oh' but a 'Yes'. Yes with a capital Y.

And then I turned to Section A.

iv

Question 10b. '"I want it recognised that sex is a subject for serious treatment and also for comic treatment: this latter aspect of it is usually ignored." Discuss E. M. Forster's novels in the light of this statement.'

Sebastian is probably handling this one. Hopefully in person and not in the light of E. M. Forster's novels. Not in the light at all.

It is four-thirty p.m. on the first day. Slowly (I am still prone upon the sofa) the sub-text of this novel, Novel Paper is coming clear.

It is not our intelligence that is being tested here, nor even our powers of decision making — though seven hours have elapsed and I have not yet decided which questions to answer, if answer there is. No. Secretly the English Department is in the employ of the Psychology Department where they are making a study of human responses to time. This method is cheaper than sending us off into space, even though I notice, reading question 14a while levitating a little off the sofa, that something has happened to gravity. Or else I am a victim of conspiracy theories.

Question 14a. 'This eternal time-question is accordingly, for the novelist, always there and always formidable.' (Henry James)

And here is time again, outcropping in Question 11. '.... in the twentieth century, the notion of "reality" on which the novel's realism was based, is called more and more into question...'

A pause. An aside. I am not a hundred percent certain that I am in the twentieth century. Read on, Macduff.

'Any man of real individuality tries to know and understand what is happening, even in himself, as he goes along. This struggle for verbal consciousness should not be left out in art. It is a very great part of life. It is the passionate struggle into conscious being.' (D. H. Lawrence).

For fictional purposes I have edited this question. The quotation is longer and duller than that but I am trying to understand what is happening even in myself. I have trouble not only raising my self into conscious being but raising myself out of the sofa.

Seven times the paper asks us to discuss something 'in the light of.' (Hyperbole. For seven read four).

It is growing dark. I fictionalise. It is only May, remember, and 5.30 in the afternoon. Do not worry. We do not have to plod, chronologically through the next forty hours. This is not *Tristram Shandy*. I can do a literary leap or five. There is probably a technical term for this which Pipforth would know. Analepsis. Prolepsis. Flashing backwards and forwards. Can one do this with centuries?

You will be wanting to know what has happened to Jane, Alice, Peter and Sebastian. And I shall have to make it up. It is post-modernist practice to deny authorial omniscience and to keep reminding the reader that he/she is reading fiction.

Jane, orderly, efficient Jane, has finished the entire paper and gone for a swim.

Sebastian is reading *Dombey and Son* which he has never read before. He has one hundred and twenty-two pages to go.

Alice has not drowned herself and will stay up all night, writing. There is no question on *Middlemarch*.

Peter is out cold. He will not begin answering any questions until the forty-second hour.

None of us has fallen in love, died, given birth or stopped eating. Sometimes it is amazing how little can happen in forty-eight hours.

vi

3 a.m. Wednesday, May 22nd.

The use of diaries and letters is a narrative trick that allows an author to jump about in time. The action can be condensed, long descriptions avoided, a sense of the letter-writer's character conveyed by voice. (cf. Austen). The diary device is a splendid vehicle for communicating a character's inner monologue, the 'flow of interior consciousness' as Lawrence would have it.

I have to end here. I am sorry to leave you *in medias res* (see epic) as it were. I like a story with a beginning, a middle and an end myself. I know how you feel. But I need to begin. The Novel Paper that is.

I am back at my desk. I have a bowl of cornflakes to hand. I am considering the following statement: 'Truth uncompromisingly told will always have its ragged edges.' (Herman Melville).

Well, if you insist…

*

Once upon a time I had a tutor who had the most beautiful pair of hands ever attached to a man's arms. And on one finger of one hand he had a beautiful ring. (This is immaterial). Well then, once upon the aforementioned time when I was searching for my soul in the pages of Jung, addling my brains with Kierkegaard and when, dearly beloved, the night, metaphorically, was very dark indeed and I happened to mention this, casually, en passant, well then, he of the beautiful hands waved one of them (I think it was his left) in the air, and said, 'Lizzie, trust to the poets.'

And so I did and I do. And I came home, happy ever after and was reunited with my family and knew that Wyatt was before Donne.

There! Will that do? Now I am going to start the Novel Paper. Now? Yes.

◆ After the Snow Queen ◆

THE GOODNESS OF GERDA ROSE was enough to sink the heart. It was both relentless and effortless. It was as if The Fall had never happened, or if it had, Gerda had missed it. She was still in the Garden of Eden, in love with her childhood sweetheart, Kay. At forty-five, for heaven's sake!

Only now, and at long last, she was about to marry him and Madge, Jude and I were guests at the wedding. Back in our schooldays, the three of us had spent hours talking about Gerda, wondering what would make her crack — lose her temper, cheat, forget her homework, arrive late, appear with dirty nails. And later on, in our teens and twenties, we were still wondering, only now we wondered when, if ever, Gerda would lose her virginity, fall in lust and, above all, give up on Kay Frost.

Over the years Gerda's life of goodness was a constant reminder of the mess we'd made of ours — Jude, twice divorced, Madge apparently addicted to unrequited love and alcohol, and me. Any book of judgement might say I'd betrayed one member of my family after another, even if I might argue that I'd had good reasons. Meanwhile Gerda had cleaned cathedrals and lived on a pittance, worked with refugees, carried banners that said 'Peace Not War' and stayed in love with Kay.

We'd had long, and usually rather drunken debates, about whether Gerda was truly good or simply 'nice'. Often the argument concerned Gerda's taste — or lack of.

'Remember her bedroom?' Madge asked. 'Still full of teddies when she was twenty-five. And the wallpaper! Roses, roses, roses.' It was Madge's contention that no-one with such an awful lack of taste and style could possibly be good.

Jude, who at school had had something of a crush on Gerda and never entirely got over it, said style and taste had nothing to do with it. Gerda had been, was and always would be, good at heart.

'Well then, goodness is frightfully unattractive,' said Madge. She blamed Gerda's granny. 'She never let her grow up,' she said. 'Gerda was still in vests and socks when we were into thongs and bikini waxing.'

'But so pretty,' said Jude. 'I used to think she looked as if she'd walked out of a fairy tale — so dreamy and willowy and with all that fly-away hair.'

In our thirties we'd mostly given up on Gerda, unable to cope, I suspect, with this saintly exemplum in our lives. There was the odd phone call in which one or other of us had heard that Gerda was in Peru, looking after street children, or she'd rushed to rescue Kay, post divorce, post breakdown, post one disaster or another. There were plenty of those.

Now here we all were, up from London, drinking gin in a village pub in Cumbria, an hour before Gerda's marriage to Kay. The church, just down the road, was one of those small, Saxon numbers you might find on a calendar and send at Christmas to an ex-pat friend in Saudi or Dubai. And of course none of us had been able to resist the invitation.

'Well, here's to her,' I said. 'She's got her man at last.'

'Though what she ever saw in him, I'll never know,' said Madge. 'He was a cold fish, if ever there was.'

'Gerda said he had a little splinter of ice in his heart,' I said. 'But it didn't seem to bother her. She said it was sure to melt.'

'She always believed in the happy-ever-after ending,' said Jude. All three of us, I thought, had given up on Happy-Ever-After and settled for Surviving-Somehow. It's hard to be happy about someone else's happy ending. Jude, generous and romantic, obviously could and Madge, as obviously, couldn't.

'Well, she's had to wait a long time for her happy ending,' Madge said now, rattling the ice in her glass. 'Most people get over their first loves. They don't stalk them half way round the world. The life Kay's had has probably left him bald, pot-bellied, penniless and worn-out.'

'I heard he'd inherited money from an aunt,' said Jude. 'Anyway, even if he hadn't, Gerda would probably rescue him. She was always trying to save him from something.'

'Mostly blondes,' said Madge. Remember the one we called the Snow Queen? Swedish girl. Permanently wrapped in furs. Kay lived with her for about a year. She had some freezing barn of a place. Far north. Kay got pneumonia twice.'

'And that splinter of ice in his heart,' said Jude.

'Well that's what Gerda claimed,' said Madge. 'She said that's why she tracked him down and broke it up. How did she do it, d'you think? Perhaps asked to borrow him for the weekend or kidnapped him by sledge.'

'They were bonded from childhood,' Jude protested. 'Soul mates. Kay just didn't recognise it.' There had to be romance in Jude's life, even if it wasn't her own.

'And then there was Bobby,' persisted Madge. 'Bobby Forester. Now she was the real love of Kay's life. If you ask me, Kay's spent his life escaping.'

'From Gerda?' asked Jude, looking pained.

'From goodness,' said Madge.

At that, and as if in answer, the church bells began to ring.

'How on earth has she managed to arrange a church wedding with someone twice divorced?' asked Jude.

'Goodness knows!' replied Madge, cramming her hat on and knocking back the last of her gin, and we all giggled. Or rather, cackled, because that's what giggles turn into come forty-plus.

'You could try to look pleased,' I told Madge as we trooped over to the church. There was no need to say this to Jude. For Jude this wedding had the quality of a fairy-tale come true. She'd dressed accordingly in a flower trimmed hat and a floaty silk coat such as one of the flower fairies might have worn if they ever wore coats. Madge, by contrast, was looking louche, in a very expensive and obviously much worn suit, a velvet scarf and a felt hat. She could have walked out of a D.H. Lawrence novel. If style and taste equalled goodness, which I doubted, Madge had it.

There were not a great many guests. Glancing round, I had the notion that those on Gerda's side of the church looked — apart from us perhaps — particularly pious. I half expected to see Gerda's granny, rosy cheeked and triumphant, but of course she was long dead. By contrast, those on Kay's side of the church looked interestingly dissolute. I remembered then that Gerda had talked Kay out of studying science ('bad for the soul') and into literature and that for a time he'd written a rather tawdry gossip column for one of the London evenings. So these could be Fleet Street folk, life-weathered, hard-drinking. And there, among them, was it … was it …? Yes!

I dug Madge in the ribs, 'Bobby Forester!' I whispered.

'And still wearing that red cap,' Madge whispered back. 'To remind him, d'you think?'

The organ struck up *Love Divine All Loves Excelling* and I sat there remembering Bobby Forester. Jude might be right, saying that Gerda was Kay's soul mate, but Madge was right too. Bobby Forester had been Kay's great passion. I saw her again as she was in our teens, hanging about street corners wearing a bomber jacket, tight jeans over tight little bum, scarlet cap, scarlet lipstick. She lived somewhere down town, one of those areas our parents were always telling us never to go, and one or other member of her family was always up in court. But what did Bobby Forester care with that lethal looking knife in her pocket which she used to take out and clean her nails? Bobby Forester with her unapologetic promiscuity, her slanty smile, her strut. She was forever taunting Kay. She'd watch him and Gerda going home from school together, hand in hand.

'Aren't you a sweetie!' she'd drawl at Kay, and the word 'sweetie' came out as a kind of insult to all masculine virility. Then she'd pocket her knife and slouch off down the street, one arm slung round some leather-jacketed thug.

Perhaps she'd really fancied Kay even then, because years later we heard they were living togther. Gerda would visit most weekends. Said they were both hopelessly impractical and needed someone to organise the house, sort out the bills etc. They weren't married, Bobby and Kay — Bobby was too much of a free spirit even to contemplate marriage. When they split up, she went off with a reindeer farmer from Lapland and Kay had a nervous breakdown. He was nursed back to health by, who else but Gerda, her reward being to see him fit and well enough to marry Harriet Brandon.

Harriet was rich, ambitious and very organised. But not domestic. Gerda would turn up with apple pies, sorbets for the freezer, bunches of roses for the hall table. Eventually there was an acrimonious divorce that left Kay homeless and out of work except, of course, that Gerda helped him get back on his feet and got him a job on some local rag. Whereupon he married the editor's secretary who rather promptly died despite Gerda's best nursing efforts. You had to wonder if destiny was saving Kay for Gerda or if Madge was right, and Kay had spent all this time escaping goodness. Goodness and Gerda. I remember a poem we'd done at school called *The Hound of Heaven*, about a man trying to run away from God.

> *I fled Him, down the nights and down the days;*
> *I fled Him down the arches of the years …*

That's how it went. Maybe that was how it had been for Kay. I could almost feel sorry for him.

The sight of Bobby Forester cheered Madge. She patted her hat and sat up straight, hopeful of a little drama, hopeful that the happy ending might not be quite so happy.

'D'you think she was invited?' she whispered. 'I bet Kay flips when he sees her.'

Jude, on the other side of me, had turned a distressed pink. 'I hope she hasn't come to make trouble,' she murmured. 'D'you thnk she still has that knife? I know she didn't really want Kay, but she didn't want anyone else to have him either.'

'Certainly not Gerda,' said Madge.

Bobby had an end of pew seat. I think all three of us suddenly imagined her rising up and stabbing Gerda as she came down the aisle.

We could only see the back of Kay. Probably to Madge's disappointment he didn't look bald, pot-bellied or worn out. On the contrary, he looked rather elegant, dressed in a classy grey flannel suit. Once, when he turned, I caught a glimpse of an exotic tie. From where I sat it looked as if roses clambered up it. Of course he didn't have the golden curls of his boy-hood, but he was slim and broad-shoul-dered. One might even call him distinguished-looking which was unfair really, as he hadn't done anything to make himself so.

Then the organ began the wedding march and we all turned to watch Gerda come down the aisle. She came alone. Obviously no-one was going to give Gerda away. She'd 'given herself' to Kay almost forty years ago.

Beside me I heard Madge groan. I wish I could be more charitable and say that Gerda looked lovely, but she didn't. She'd chosen a wedding dress that might have suited a twenty year old. Might. The dress had a huge skirt of many flounces and ribbons. The net of her veil was garnished with pearls and sequins. Under it I could just glimpse her hair, that pale-flax fly-away hair, now bleached and worn in bunches! She carried a huge bouquet of red roses. Even Jude looked somewhat stunned and across the aisle I saw Bobby Forester bend her head as if trying not to laugh.

I might have laughed myself, only at that point I looked back at Kay. I think I half expected him to bolt, to jump over the pews and run off with Bobby Forester who no doubt had a reindeer tethered outside and waiting just for this moment. Instead I saw that Kay was crying, tears running down his face so that the best man had to give him a hand-kerchief. It came back to me then, Gerda calmly saying that the splinter of ice in Kay's heart would one day melt.

This was it, then. The ice melting. Love redeeming, just as Gerda's granny had always said it would. I won't go on about the ceremony itself, except to say that both Gerda's 'I do' and Kay's 'I do' rang out loudly enough to make even the vicar look a little shaken.

Aftewards, outside the church, all three of us were waiting for Kay and Gerda's encounter with Bobby Forester. And as they headed for the car we saw her running behind them with a handful of confetti. For a moment, as she lifted her hand, I saw something flash but it was only a ring, a large icy diamond.

As the best man opened the car door, Kay and Gerda turned towards Bobby. Kay shrugged and spread out his hands, as if to say, 'what could I do?' And Gerda? Gerda put her thumb to her nose and cocked a snook!

'Well!' said Jude, slightly outraged, 'that wasn't very nice was it?'

'No, it wasn't,' said Madge happily.

All the wedding guests began heading for their own cars. I looked round to see who Bobby was with, if anyone. But she'd vanished. As we walked towards Madge's car I could have sworn I heard the thud of hooves and as we drove off I distinctly saw the tips of a pair of antlers and a scarlet cap.

♦ The Sweet Possessive ♦

YOU WOULDN'T THINK YOU could be sent to prison because of an apostrophe would you? Of course the judge didn't put it like that. Twenty eight days for disturbing the peace, is what he said. But in those twenty eight days I had time to think it all out and I know for certain that if it hadn't been for that particular apostrophe not one jot of peace would have been disturbed.

Now I admit that when it comes to apostrophes I'm, well, what Jack calls 'a bit of a junkie.' But to me that little flying comma — that's what it looks like, doesn't it, a comma up in the air — gentles life along. I mean think how sort of bossy it sounds when you say *I can not* or *I do not* and how — well , wistful, apologetic almost, it sounds when you say I can't or I don't. There's almost a *sorry* hidden inside *I can't* and *I don't*. My favourite apostrophe is the one that tells you who belongs to who or what belongs to who. And what gets me all in a tizz is when people put the apostrophe in the wrong place.

Before Jack came along you could almost say it was my hobby, going about town with my box of chalks and my marker pens, hunting down signs and rubbing out wrong apostrophes — you know like *apple-apostrophe-s* when it should be just apples — or adding an apostrophe when one's been missed out. When the weather was really bad I'd hunt them out in the newspaper. You'd be amazed how many people don't understand the apostrophe. Maybe that's another reason why I'm so fond of it. Some days I feel I'm a bit like an apostrophe myself, misunderstood, not really noticed. Or not noticed until Jack came along.

According to Jack, putting the world's apostrophes to rights wasn't just a hobby, like I thought it was, it was more like an addiction. It was like that obsessive compulsive thingy when someone can't stop washing their hands. It needed treatment, Jack said. It was a pity there wasn't something like Apostrophes Anonymous, Jack said and he laughed until he almost fell out of bed. 'One of these days,' Jack said, 'one of your greengrocers will take you to court. Damaging blackboards. Graffiti writing.'

Actually, Jack said a lot more and when I look back, I can see that some of it was quite nasty and if I didn't see it at the time it was because Jack talked in paragraphs. Some people do. Have you noticed? It's as if they've never heard of a comma or a full stop or a dash or a nice pair of brackets. Before I got hooked on apostrophes it was the dash I liked most. I thought it was kind of impetuous. I liked the look of it on the page. Well actually I like the look of most punctuation marks on the page. As a child, as soon as I discovered them, I thought they were much prettier than the alphabet. I've always wished we had those back to front question marks the Spanish have or those upside down exclamation marks. And the French have lots of extras with those cedillas they sometimes tuck under their Cs and those circumflexes that look like little dunces' caps. I've often thought it would be nice to have a curtain with a pattern of punctuation marks. Or maybe a table cloth.

Anyway, that's all by the by really. Because I fell in love with a man who talked in paragraphs, a man who seemed completely unpunctuated. Maybe it was the attraction of opposites. When a man talks in paragraphs a lot of it goes by in a blur. You can't keep up. I've wondered if there's something in the brain that actually *needs* commas and question marks. Even semi-colons. Sometimes I think it's punctuation that gives words their music. Where was I? Well, for a time, at least for the time it took for me to really hanker for that apostrophe that would make me belong to him, make me Jack apostrophe s's wife, I loved him world without end, or at least world without full stops.

And that's the crux of it really, because I wanted to marry Jack. I'd never wanted to marry anyone before — well, I'd never been in love before had I— and I knew it was rather late in the day — I'd just had my 56th birthday — and Jenny, that's my sister, talked me into internet dating. I suppose I should have realised from Jack's emails that he was an Unpunctuated Man because not only were there no commas or full stops in his emails but there were no capital letters either. At the beginning I thought it was just the kind of internet way of writing, the way you see words all run together on the side of vans like *www.livehappily-everafter.com* for a furniture company. Anyway, before we actually met, I spent quite a long time fantasising about how I'd introduce Jack to colons and semi-colons and yes, of course, the apostrophe.

And it didn't take me long after meeting him — it was always out of town which should have made me suspicious — to fall in love and once I'd fallen, well, it seemed the natural thing to want to marry him. 'Go for it girl!' Jenny said. I think that had an exclamation mark at the end of it. So that's how it was. I wanted to marry Jack. I wanted to be Jack's wife. That's Jack apostrophe s's wife. Have I said that before? I kept saying it to myself. A lot. It's important to put the apostrophe in the right place because if you put it after the s instead of before the s, it would mean there was more than one Jack. A plural of Jack. One Jack, two Jacks. Which is quite funny in a way, because that's how things turned out. One Jack, two Jacks. That's something else the apostrophe does, sorts out singular and plural. Let's not go there. That still hurts.

Where was I? Oh yes, telling you how I wanted to be Jack apostrophe s's wife. At the time it was still my very favourite apostrophe. I thought of it as the sweet possessive. Sometimes when Jack had been to stay for the weekend and left all sorts of things behind, I'd go round the house chanting, Jack's hat, Jack's toothbrush, Jack's socks, Jack's smell. Jack's. Then I put it in reverse. Hat of Jack, toothbrush of Jack, socks of Jack, smell of Jack. It's not the same is it?

Mostly if we weren't at my house, we went out into the country. Jack said I needed apostrophe protection (ha ha) because there were so many wrong ones in town and that anyway the countryside was so much more romantic wasn't it and although we were getting on a bit we could still pretend to be young lovers couldn't we and he remembered when and how and why and so on, paragraph after hypnotic paragraph in that lovely Welsh lilt he had.

It was only at weekends he came to my house. He'd turn up after dark on a Friday night. I was forever asking him to come earlier so maybe we could go out somewhere but he always said he had to work late. And then on Saturday and Sunday he was too tired to go anywhere. 'Let's just snuggle in,' he'd say. So we did and because he was with me I stopped looking in the paper for apostrophes gone wrong. (That strikes me as funny now because it wasn't apostrophes going wrong, it was me!) And of course there was no way I could go apostrophe hunting round town like I used to do in the pre-Jack days. It made me quite jumpy at first. Twitchy even. That must have been when Jack said I was an apostrophe junkie, that it was an addiction and he went on for paragraphs about addicts he had known, cures he had heard about or read about and which ones worked and which ones didn't until sometimes I fell asleep and I was quite glad I did because it relieved the twitchyness, although it occurs to me now that possibly I was getting a bit bored only I didn't like to admit it. Hark at me! I think I'm talking in paragraphs. Maybe it's catching.

It was only after a few months that I started to hint at marriage and that was because Jenny put me up to it. 'A man often needs a nudge,' was what she said, 'particularly when he's got to your Jack's age. How old is he anyway?'

'I don't know,' I said, and suddenly there was a translation in my head. 'I do not know,' I said out loud and to myself I said *there is an awful lot I do not know about Jack.*

Among the things I did not know — doesn't that sound sharp without the apostrophe that goes into didn't or don't? — was how old he was, where he lived, where he worked and why he wouldn't be seen out with me in town. In fact I could make up several unpunctuated paragraphs on the things I didn't know about Jack. Things I was soon to find out.

It was about six months after Jack and I had been going together. A Friday afternoon and I was coming back from the supermarket loaded with bags of food. I always had to stock up for the whole weekend. One way and another Jack was really costing me. Anyway, I could see this woman hanging about near the top of my street as if she was waiting for someone. Which she was. Me!

She started off all posh and polite. 'Excuse me,' she said as if she was about to ask me the way somewhere. 'Excuse me, but I'm Nan.'

'So?' I said.

'Nan,' she repeated. 'And I think you should know, I'm Jack's wife.'

I've gone over this a hundred times asking myself how I'd have acted if she'd said, *excuse me, but I think you should know that Jack is my husband.* Well, I'd have been upset, obviously. And angry, yes. But I don't think I'd have lost it, grabbing her hair, slapping her face, pouring a pint of milk over her head, screaming and kicking so that someone — Amy Rice, I think, any kind of trouble's a magnet to Amy — called the police. You see what made me flip, what made me see red, what set about five exclamation marks dancing in front of my eyes, was that apostrophe. The one I think of as the sweet possessive. Jack apostrophe s, Jack's wife. The very title I'd had in mind for myself.

So you see that's why I think it's the apostrophe that's to blame for my twenty-eight days in prison and I suppose it was a kind of cure because afterwards I thought I'd do what Jenny suggested and maybe take up a new hobby, yoga or pilates or something — anything to distract me from punctuation in general and apostrophes in particular.

Anyway, there's a kind of jolly ending to all this. Because about six months after I'd come out of clink and taken up car maintenance (not that I've got a car but I like tinkering with all the things inside an engine) I met Nan again. It was at Tesco's in town and she had this not-Jack man pushing her trolley.

I was about to go past her, nose in the air so to speak, when she stopped me, putting her hand on my arm. 'I thought you'd like to know that I'm not Jack's wife any more. I'm Jack's ex.'

Quick as a flash and brushing her hand off my arm, I said 'You and me both then!'

Though even now it strikes me as odd that somehow that apostrophe still attaches both of us to Jack. And I thought that maybe Nan was Jack's weekday wife, and for just a little while I was sort-of Jack's weekend wife. Two Jacks. A plural of Jacks and now both of us Jack's exes. That gentle apostrophe, see, showing that once upon a time we'd both belonged to Jack.

◆ The Proposal ◆

O<small>N SUNDAY THE SAILOR CAME.</small> Rosa gave us our instructions. My mother was not to laugh too loudly. I was to mind my manners.

The sailor came for tea. None of the others — the men in love with Rosa — had ever been invited for tea. They called to take her to dances. They stood on the doorstep in mackintoshes that had been wrung in a mangle of anguish. They had pale yellow hair that flopped with exhausted passion. The tips of their collars curled with anxiety; they dangled scarves of longing, they had pale blue eyes and lacked chins.

Rosa made them wait on the doorstep and then swept past them wearing my mother's black velvet honeymoon cloak. (It was full of moth holes, but you'd never know). She walked with her arms stretched before her like a sleep walker. This was because her nail varnish wasn't dry but it gave added drama to the honeymoon cloak.

But on Sunday the sailor came for tea and Rosa — my proud ocean-liner of a sister, who every morning set sail for the city in a smart black suit with velvet lapels — Rosa, six foot tall, Brunhilde-breasted and disdainful — oh, something awful had happened to Rosa.

The scorn had gone out of her. Her scarlets and blacks had dimmed overnight. For tea with the sailor she wore a soft lilac wool dress and a shawl. Sweet pink lipstick. Sweet pink nail varnish.

When the sailor arrived I frisked him for faults. There weren't any. He was as tall, blonde and handsome as any magazine hero. It was sickening. Within half an hour my mother said, 'You can call me Momma', and he did so, easily, as though he travelled all over the world calling strange old women 'Momma'.

I sat at the table and was ashamed. I was eleven.

'Momma' and Rosa and the sailor all chattered away; my father silently hunched himself over his plate of ham and salad and forked it in, fast, as he usually did. I wondered if he was ashamed too.

For tea there was white bread and butter cut in minute triangles and with the crusts removed for decency's sake. And there was one of my mother's trifles which was basically swiss roll soaked in sherry and smeared with custard. After tea the sailor asked if he might talk to my father. Alone. My father pretended surprise. Under cover of the table cloth he had undone his belt. Now he hitched his trousers up and shambled into the front room. The sailor followed.

Rosa helped my mother with the dishes and my mother pretended that this was normal.

It was raining outside. I got out my box of paper dolls and sat under the table with them. I'd nearly given them up, but not quite. I made the chief girl doll have a row with the chief boy doll. She called him a beast and he called her a horror. I wished I knew some really rude words, but I only knew 'bugger' and was confused about the word's gender.

I wondered what was going on in the front room. I imagined that my father would stand there looking big and grand and in an awful voice he would say, 'AND DO YOU LOVE MY DAUGHTER?' all in capitals. And the sailor would go down on one knee and answer him with tears in his eyes and a catch in his throat. And after that I wasn't sure whether my father ought to pour champagne over the sailor's head or tap him on the shoulder with a sword or whether he just said, 'ARISE — SON!'

After a while there was the sound of laughter from the front room and the door of the drinks cupboard being opened and then my father came to the door and shouted 'Momma!' My mother and Rosa went into the front room and there was more laughter and kissing and glasses clinking.

I put on my mac then and went down to the sea. It was still raining and the wind was fierce but I didn't care. Everything was on the move. Sky, clouds, sea. Everything was wild. Untamed.

It was late autumn and the Council had got the sand bags lined up along the sea wall. Sometime soon the sea would fling itself at that sandbagged wall like a mad grey cat that's been shut in one room too long. Every year the sea won, flooding over the wall, the sandbags — sometimes sweeping into the ground floor of the houses.

I walked up and down the deserted promenade with its empty shelters where the old folk liked to sit of an afternoon or where, at night, young couples 'canoodled'. 'Canoodled' was my mother's word. It made me think of the cooing of wood pigeons in our back garden. The word — a tender, nestling, nesting word — was a cross between a cuddle and a coo. I hated it. Once caught in a canoodle, I thought, and you'd never get out again.

The sea was practising its winter high jumps. The wind howled like my heart. I leant against the railings and let wind and sea salt sting my cheeks, my nose, the tips of my ears. I wanted to shout back at the sea. Wanted to say 'Take him, this sailor of yours! He belongs to you. Take him!'

'And drown him,' said a very small voice inside me. And once I'd thought that, I thought how easy it would be. How often had I heard the life-boat go out to a ship in trouble?

Sailors drowned every day of the week didn't they? At school we sang

> *Oh hear us when we cry to Thee*
> *For those in peril on the sea*

at morning assembly. I sang it now, to myself, silently, conjuring up a distant storm-tossed ship, an arm raised helplessly from the waves ....

It would take only one voyage. One voyage before the wedding. Drowned sailors went straight to heaven, I was certain of it. O Lord, I prayed, let him go on one more voyage. And I pictured myself comforting Rosa in her bereavement.

And then I was afraid. Afraid of Rosa. For she would know, of course, in that uncanny way she had of reading my mind, that it was all my fault, that it was I who'd called up the storm and drowned her love. Rosa might be all lilac and pink now, but I knew she was scarlet and black at heart. Once, in a huge rage, she'd stung my legs all over with nettles. No, I didn't fear my prayer being answered nearly as much as I feared Rosa's revenge.

When I got home again she and the sailor had gone for a drive. (Or for a 'canoodle' I thought miserably.) My mother was angry with me for going out 'just in that thin mac', my father was deep in the Sunday papers as unbothered as if he acquired a son-in-law every day of the week. As if it wouldn't change things forever.

The next day I tried to tell Anna about Rosa and the sailor. I wish I could say Anna was my best friend, but she wasn't. She was Penelope's. I hoped to inherit her. I'd been working on it for months. Anna had thick fair plaits, a sea-captain for father, and a scar on her knee from an adventure. You couldn't look at Anna without thinking of adventure.

'Rosa's engaged,' I told her when we sat on the playing field at lunch time with our gymslips wound round our legs to hide our navy knickers from the grammar school boys who leered at us over the fence.

'You'll have her bedroom when she gets married,' said Anna who didn't have her own room and was obsessed by territory.

'Don't want it!'

'*And* you'll be an Auntie,' Anna added encouragingly, 'when she has babies that is. Imagine being an Auntie when you're only eleven or twelve!'

'Who wants to be an auntie?' I cried desperately.

'Don't you like him?' asked Anna curiously, 'Your Rosa's fella — what's the matter with him?'

'Nothing!'

How could I explain that that was precisely what the matter with him was? That he was faultless. That I'd have felt a lot better if he had a hump back or a boil on his neck or six hidden wives.

'You're jealous then,' said Anna.

'I'm not!

'Y'are!'

'Not!'

'Y'are!'

It was impossible! I wanted to try and tell Anna how I thought Rosa was special, but I didn't know how to say it without sounding boastful. I wanted to say that I thought Rosa had destiny, that although other, average girls had to be sweet and kind, lilac and pink, it was Rosa's destiny to sail double-deckers into town, Boadicea of the top deck, inviolate, triumphant, wild and free as the sea.

She was a pagan, our Rosa. Black and imperious, fierce,

nettle-stinging and fine. And the sailor, pale, blonde and meek was a Christianising influence. Devitalising. Boadicea would no more crack her whip; caught in a canoodle she would bend her head. Tamed. It was sad.

The day after I'd tried and failed to communicate all this to Anna I got bronchitis. My mother said it was going out in a thin mac on a cold Sunday afternoon.

My temperature rose like the sea trying to leap the sandbags. For the first feverish two days I could think of nothing but the next breath. It was a relief.

On the third day I woke at dawn. I could breathe again. The whole world seemed at peace, purged, like my lungs, like my thoughts, of evil. I imagined that all the murderers, burglars and baddies had crept out of town with their badness on their backs like coalmen of the night.

I spent the week enjoying the small tyranny and regular visitors due to the convalescent. My father came and stood, awkward and embarrassed in the doorway. Doctor Lottie came with the white hairs of her nostrils trembling like antennae and prescribed awful smelling poultices for my back and chest. Mrs Potts, my mother's best friend, came and told me tales of when she was a little girl and at the exciting bits closed her eyes for so long you thought she was dying with the loveliness of it all.

And of course Rosa came. She came after work, wearing the black suit with the velvet lapels and her scarlet lipstick. Rosa had never done the motherly bit and she didn't start now. She prowled around my room for a while idly picking up books, reading the labels on the medicine, looking at things I'd stuck on the walls. Eventually she stood at the foot of the bed, head on one side and scrutinised me as if I was something in a shop window she was deciding would or wouldn't do.

'We'll have to do something with your hair,' she said, coming close up, tilting my chin then tugging one of my thin plaits. 'You can't be a bridesmaid like that. You look like Little Orphan Annie.'

'Don't want to be a bridesmaid,' I wheezed with an attempt at rebellion. It had come back, with a sudden hot feverishness, how I'd walked along the sea front praying that the sailor would drown. It wasn't in church, of course, and I hadn't prayed out loud. But in my heart I'd prayed 'O hear us when we cry to Thee, for those in peril on the sea'. Peril was what I'd prayed for secretly, silently. With such evil in my heart how could I be a bridesmaid? Could prayers work backwards, I wondered, and the Lord strike me dead as I walked behind Rosa up the aisle? Or more appropriately, the ground open and swallow me up in ocean. Who knew what perils the Lord could prepare?

Rosa raised her eyebrows. Her nose became thin and imperious. She seemed taller than ever, as if she was growing in front of me. 'You *will* be a bridesmaid!' she commanded, 'Like it or not! Who the hell else have I got?' Then she stalked angrily to the door, her ankle bones cracking with temper. All scarlet and black again.

Hardly was I well again and back at school than all the preparations for the wedding began.

My father was going to make it a grand affair. He'd booked a hotel with chandeliers dripping from the ceiling. He had silver-edged wedding invitations printed. He planned a wedding breakfast of salmon and turkey and peaches. There would be free cigars at the end. An orchestra. Dancing. It was not so much a wedding reception as a statement of wealth and success.

My mother bought a grey silk dress with tiny pearls all over the breast and a hat of grey and pink feathers. She looked pretty as a bird. My grandfather hired top hat and tails from Moss Bros and looked like the man who broke the bank at Monte Carlo.

Rosa personally cut off my stringy plaits. To everyone's surprise my hair curled. It curled all over my head in the most angelic way possible. I was transformed.

Rosa bought me a dress of pink satin and white net. I had a single rose with trailing satin ribbons as a head-dress, silver ballet slippers and a Nell Gwyn basket of flowers.

I put them all on and stood looking at myself in the mirror. Stormy seas, perilous voyages, drowned sailors, vanished from my mind. I was curly-headed, innocent, eleven — and a bridesmaid.

♦ Female Company ♦

S O ALL ON A MONDAY morning-oh, here I am dusting the velvet seat of my Victorian chair for Jerome's immaculate bottom and wearing my long dress.

Monday morning is Jerome's morning. The first Monday in every month belongs to Jerome. He's my head-man, soul-man, my juggler of thoughts, my unshrinkable Shrink.

Soon as I woke up I remembered it was Monday, *the* Monday, the Monday we've been heading towards for two whole years. Today I'm to go out.

I haven't left this house — this old, thick-walled house — for two years.

We've been practising for today's Outing. Under hypnosis Jerome has been taking me on an imaginary journey down the hall, out of the imaginary front door, down the imaginary garden. Inch by inch, foot by foot we go — his foot, my foot, his foot my foot — on to the end of the imaginary path, out of the gate and away to the lake.

Today's the day we convert imagination to reality. No more pretending. Today is for real.

For months now both Jerome and Ivor have been full of optimism about my little amble. I'm like a car they've built together and now plan to try on the road. Such pleasure they've had discussing the technical details of what they refer to as 'Annie's hysterical phobia — Annie's agor-agor-agora-phobia'. You could say it's bonded them. And this morning, this very special Monday morning, will show the result of all their efforts. Give a roll on the drums! Give a Taa-raa-ra-BOOM-de-eh! And Annie of the phobic hysterics will walk forth. A woman of the world again.

It'll be a triumph for both of them. A successful case-study for Jerome. The restoration of his outgoing — *outgoing* ha! — wife for Ivor. I love them both. Ivor, urgent and intense, Jerome wry, slow and detached. I've no choice but to indulge them.

When I woke up this morning I felt neither fear nor excitement. Ivor was still asleep. I curled up round him. Ivor only lets me cuddle when he's asleep. Awake he says he can't think properly when someone's touching him. Asleep, Ivor is warm and beautiful. His body has an earth heat I'd like to burrow into. I curled round him trying to absorb enough heat to last me through the day, wishing that I could lie like that for ever and ever. Or perhaps that Ivor could, because once Ivor's awake he sheds me like his pyjamas.

I'm always jealous that Ivor should wake up and immediately find himself. His physical being seems to be standing beside his bed like a shop-dummy, all ready for Ivor to step into. My own being seems painfully scattered like items of clothing left about the room after a hurried undressing.

When Ivor comes downstairs for breakfast he looks as if he has scrubbed me away with his toothpaste. Even the expression on his face is dressed, dressed for the world out there — and all of him, his sharp white shirt cuffs, the polished caps of his shoes, the crease of his trousers, the neat knot of his tie, all these thing deny me.

But this morning Ivor offers to stay around. If I need him. If it would help. I know he doesn't mean it. Every bone in his body is tense with the desire to be off. Out of this old dark house. Away in his bright, practical office. And after all, what is he paying Jerome for?

I want to tell Ivor that I don't want to go out. Not today. Not ever. But I can't. After he's gone, blowing me a kiss then giving me a thumbs up sign, I begin tidying and cleaning the house, ready for Jerome. Listening all the time. I have learnt to listen.

I have an intimate knowledge of this house. I know it as well as a lover knows the body of the beloved. I know the outlines, the shapes and surfaces of the walls and floors. I know exactly where the sun falls and where the shadows lie. I know all the marks, stains, the pieces of falling plaster, the cracks in the ceilings. Most of all I know the voices of the women.

There are seven women who have lived in this house since it was built in 1750. There was Annie — Annie the first, whose initial is inscribed on a heart on the front of the house together with an H for her Hugh. So. Annie, then Olwen, Hetty, Jane, Annie-the-second, Sarah, Elizabeth and now me.

I think of them now as *my* women, although for the first year here I refused to acknowledge them. Of course I knew there was something about the house. It was like a trip wire. I'd come rushing in, about to do something, attend to some task — make a phone call, peel the potatoes — and then stop. Because there was a peculiar brand of silence in the house. A new silence, as if someone had just finished speaking and the air had not yet had time to settle, was still disturbed, still reverberating.

Also — and perhaps this does seem like madness — the inside of the house seemed to have the ability to weigh matters, to differentiate between the irrelevant and the important. The trivial, spoken thoughts seemed to bounce off the walls, while the unspoken ones — the thoughts of the heart — were immediately soaked up, absorbed into the walls of the house. As if — as if the walls were — well, *thirsty.*

It was disconcerting — to say the least. I found myself leaving sentences trailing in mid-air, abandoning ideas when the house chilled them. I had to learn silence. And only then did I begin to listen to the women. Only then did their presence seep into me so that…

So that now I am heavy with them — with their loves and their griefs, the bearing of their children, the burial of their dead. I no longer feel like a solitary person. I am part of a chain — Annie-the-third, the next in line.

It took me months to be able to hear the women clearly. Their conversation is horribly limited. They talk of nothing but men, marriage, babies, loving, dying. Were they my contemporaries I should soon be more than a little irritated. But because they are only ghosts, because their voices have that lingering, pervasive quality of ghosts, their words make poems in my head. Love poems, love songs.

It seems that before, I was empty of these. I'd a head full of information. Thoughts and ideas culled from books, school, university. But no poems. No songs. No *inner* world.

Day after day Annie-the-first would sit in the bedroom rocker saying, 'I'm waiting for Hughie to come home. He'll be home on the hour.' She speaks so complacently, the first Annie. And Olwen, drifting round the room, would say, 'Megan was born here first, and then Roland. As broad as he was long, was Roland.' And on they would go, the two of them, not minding me a bit as I moved between them, putting away the clothes in the chest of drawers, pulling up the bed, opening the windows, dusting. Sometimes Olwen would absent-mindedly help, though Annie never did.

For me these women have become — well, it will be obvious by now — my only reality.

When I told Jerome about them, he was not impressed. He'd heard it all before, I suppose — voices, hauntings, his stock-in-trade. Dear Jerome! Those large, raw hands on his knees, when he sits in the Victorian chair. Upright and

reputation, his own wobbly grip on reality — all these blocked him.

'Ah,' he said, 'I see you're dressed for an occasion. And this morning's walk is definitely an occasion.'

I knew then that this was an ending, that Jerome would have to go and go without knowing he was going and that he would never come back.

He perched briefly on the edge of the chair, determined not to settle. 'It's all going to go well this morning,' he said in his best reassuring voice. 'It's a lovely morning. As lovely as your dress.'

I looked down at the dress. It was a pale lilac silk with a lace collar, probably made in the twenties. I'd bought it years ago. Two pounds at an Oxfam shop.

'The dress is wrong,' I said. 'I'll have to change.'

Jerome looked doubtful. I knew what he was thinking. That I was trying to put off the moment, that I was capable of making excuses that lasted all morning.

'All right,' he said. 'But be quick.'

I started up the stairs. 'Annie!' Jerome called after me, 'For God's sake don't make me come and get you.'

'I won't,' I called back.

Annie-the-first was sitting on the edge of the bed.

'*You* are going out with Jerome,' I said, 'and you're going to be me. You'll take him to the lake.'

It was all very easy. I dressed Annie in my brown coat and beret. Both smelt a bit.

Annie doesn't really look like me. She's the same build, but her hair is brown and her face much thinner. The beret covered her hair. When she was dressed and I'd made her stop giggling, I called down the stairs to Jerome.

'Jerome — promise me something!'

I could hear him pacing the living room.

'If I can,' he said carefully.

'Don't look at me until we reach the lake.'

'Do you look very funny?'

'Very!'

'All right then, I won't look.' I sent Annie down then. I could tell by the stiffness in Jerome's voice that he was keeping his promise. He was not looking.

'I'd like to hold your hand, Annie,' he said, 'but that wouldn't do. There — it's a lovely morning. It ought to be your loveliest morning. We are going to walk down to the lake and back again. It will take ten minutes.'

I heard Jerome opening the hall door, the porch door, the front door. He closed it very gently. I heard their footsteps going down the path and then the gate click open and shut.

Annie began to say something but I couldn't catch the words. I knew it would be all right. I knew she wouldn't bring Jerome back.

I went downstairs and poured myself a stiff drink. When I went back to the bedroom Olwen was there. She was making the bed, plumping up the pillows. Big, fat downy pillows.

Olwen turned round when she felt me there. She smiled. Rather sadly I thought. 'I'll look after Ivor,' she said.

◆ Snow ◆

WE ARE ALL BORN WITH A CHIP of ice in the heart. I imagine it forming — a thin, translucent sliver — the moment the umbilical cord is cut. It is the chill of the heart recognising its life-long solitary state. And what do we die of if not the cold? Call it whatever medical term you like. Ultimately it is the chip of ice growing, as icebergs grow, and inexorably taking over the heart.

Sometimes, lying in bed at night, I try to assess the size of the iceberg in my own heart. It is not the coldness of my feet that informs me of the state of affairs. Rather I take the pulse of my spirits, and find them low. Spring doesn't lift them as it used to do. Nor does the sight of a pretty girl. And then there is the test of compassion. Do I feel it much, reading, in the newspapers, of famine or disaster; seeing a starving child gazing out at me from the television, eyes enormous in a fleshless skull? No. A tremor perhaps. An impotent dull ache, over almost as soon as it's begun.

Down in the kitchen there's a tray of pills and potions. They might keep me going for a while. But nothing will stop the ice — the ice that stops the blood as surely as it stops love — from killing me.

And if Ruth's ghost is out there somewhere, I expect she is laughing at me and saying that this is justice, that death by ice is what I deserve.

It was the winter of '81 that Ruth died. At the inquest the coroner said that she must have lost her bearings in the snow. It was, after all, the worst winter we'd had for eighty years — or so the newspapers said. I remember how on that day the radio advised people to stay at home.

There were reports of old ladies dying of hypothermia and a postman turned to stone on his round. The drifts were so bad that even though she was only a mile from home all familiar landmarks would have been obliterated — so the coroner said.

But I knew better. Or rather I knew Ruth better. I knew the horror she had for the kind of tragedy that is sharpened by the irony of time — the saving letter that arrives a day late; the food truck appearing minutes after the starving child has died; the ship that sinks in sight of port. One of the last entries in her diary is a quotation from a book on pilotage — 'Many fine ships, many gallant men, have been lost when their destination was actually in sight. Full fathom five is no more than thirty feet.'

Was this in her mind that afternoon when she plunged out into the snow, saying she'd suffocate, suffocate, suffocate, if she stayed inside a moment longer? I shall never know.

What I do know is that I could have gone to find her. And didn't. And that since then the ice in my own heart has grown daily, as if I am suffering, during the slow torture of years, what she suffered in a brief few hours.

Let me tell you of the day. Our village is down in a valley. The hill out of it was quite impassable. The road had become like a massive coal-shoot down which the sky had tumbled sacks and sacks of snow. Enough to bury us.

The milk was brought in by a tractor that morning. I went out in my wellingtons to fetch it and walked to the bottom of the hill to confirm what was already obvious — that there was no way I would get to work that day.

To me, being cut-off was a relief — a delight. I remember how the whiteness pleased me, as if all yesterdays had been wiped out and today was the proverbial blank sheet. The shapes of the snow-drifts pleased me too — their soft lines, the way swags of snow re-shaped the road, vanquished flatness and straightness and replaced these with the aesthetic of crescents and rounds, hollows and humps. Snow flung up against the fences froze into waves. I saw only the aesthetics of snow. Not the terror of it. Looking up towards the fields — the fields where Ruth walked that afternoon — I saw that all the usual boundary lines had vanished. No-one owned anything any more. It was all one.

I see now how different it was for Ruth. One man's liberation is another man's gaol. To be cut-off meant freedom for me. To Ruth it was an imprisonment. She was imprisoned with me in what — as I learnt later from her diary — she regarded as a deathly marriage, a marriage as suffocating as the snow that bound us all in that January day and kept her from her lover.

There are nights now when I wonder about Ruth's lover and it comes over me, morbidly, I know, that it wasn't really Jim Forster she loved, but death itself. That there is some awful affinity between so-called romantic love and death, as if the desire for both is characterised by a kind of hopeless longing that can never be satisfied.

You note that I say 'so-called' romantic love. I have never felt this myself. Not the grand passion — the Antony and Cleopatra, Troilus and Crisseyde kind of stuff. Nor, to be honest have I ever wanted to. It strikes me as wholly disruptive of one's life, leads to inevitable disaster and has no lasting comfort about it. Perhaps you might think that I was born with a larger than normal chip of ice in my heart and you might be right. I'm a psychologist. I know all about the evasions of the human heart. I regard falling-in-love as one of them.

Yet I have no doubt that I loved Ruth. Truly loved her, according to my understanding of the word 'love'. She was just twenty when I married her and I some fifteen years older. It is true that I'd begun to find life inconvenient without a partner. Tiresome even. It seemed to me I had a lot to give. Not only the material things like the house (Georgian), a goodly income (I'd acquired some profitable shares over the years) but those more abstract things like loyalty, understanding, good humour. I pride myself on my humour. Ruth's father had died that year. In retrospect I can see that she sought a replacement. I can also see that I was happy to fill that role.

I am past the bitterness of thinking that I gave Ruth everything a woman could want. That awful period when one does the accounts of love. Sees the credits. Cannot understand the large minus on the other side.

What Ruth wanted, what I couldn't give her — what it was beyond any husband to give her — was longing. Longing itself. Hopeless longing. Why do I think she recognised this, that afternoon, rushing out in the snow, poorly dressed for it in her rather worn duffle coat and no hat? Why do I think it was this, and not the loss of Jim Forster, that caused her to lie down in the snow and let the late afternoon's blizzard come over her?

There are ways of losing one's bearings. That's what I've often wished I'd said to the coroner. I have noticed with some of my patients that it is unwise to cure them of their deepest neurosis. It is by these that they negotiate life. Without them they are in a landscape without signposts.

The letter from Forster came a week after the inquest. (The post, like everything else, was delayed by snow). It was post-marked Amsterdam. By then I'd found Ruth's flight ticket and the bundle of letters from Forster. The note prepared for me was a strange one. There were two quotations. (She knew my fondness for these. I am prone to collecting apt ones for my essays for *The Psychological Review*.)

'Love is not consolation, it is light', was the first. 'The state of falling-in-love is a distortion of vision that is illuminating', was the second.

My immediate reaction was one of cold rage that even her death didn't diminish. There was something so pious about those quotations. Something pious, foolish — and yes, perhaps painfully innocent. I had no difficulty in accepting both quotations. Had Ruth thought I would?

It is too late now to tell her what I do believe, which is that there cannot be constant light. That consolation should not be despised. That illumination cannot be a permanent state of the mind or the heart and that to hanker for this and this only can only lead to despair. But she no longer needs telling. She met despair that afternoon. Forster's penultimate letter makes that clear. A one-line ultimatum. 'If you are not on the plane I will know it is over'.

No way she could contact him, flying in from Athens. No way she could get to the airport. No way he could know it was over in a way he hadn't expected. 'Many fine men, many gallant ships, have been lost when their destination was actually in sight. Full fathom five is no more than thirty feet.' Less, in Ruth's case. Only a few feet of snow encased her, coffin like, when the police dogs found her.

*

If it hadn't been for Geoff Waddington, I would probably have gone on and on wondering if Ruth had died of — as romantic fiction would have it — a broken heart. Or if, as the coroner believed, in a state of distress, she had lost her bearings. Or if, as my own rather satisfactory analysis suggested, she had suddenly recognised and obeyed a deeply held death wish.

I've a lot of time for Geoff Waddington, our local vet.

He's an abrupt, compassionate, hard-drinking man. Too much tenderness in him, I've often thought. Over the years we've met at a variety of local functions. Ruth liked him too. Said the local GP could learn a lot from him.

Geoff Waddington was the last to see her. I knew this from the inquest. What I didn't know — what Waddington didn't reveal at the inquest — was the conversation they'd had.

Waddington and Ruth must have been the only two people out in the fields that afternoon. Waddington had walked to a farm to help in the difficult birth of a calf. He'd gone out well-equipped for the weather — thigh high boots, a small flask of brandy in his pocket and in any case, he knew the fields around here like the back of his hand.

He'd spotted Ruth, he told me, from some distance. She had crossed several fields and was up the far hill where an enormous pylon stands, its lines of wires stretching in every direction.

'She looked as if she was praying,' he said. We were in the kitchen. I'd noticed on previous occasions that Waddington was uneasy in either the sitting room or study. He liked the kitchen table and a glass of whisky on it. He now had both.

'Praying,' he said again, 'as if — as if the pylon was a kind of pagan totem pole. Staring up at it. Arms stretched out. Humming.'

'Humming?' I repeated.

Waddington took another gulp of his whisky. I realised then just how much the encounter with Ruth had disturbed him. And Waddington is not a man to be easily disturbed. It's probably the reason Ruth and I liked him so much. Nothing in the range of human emotions fazed Waddington.

'The wires hum,' said Waddington. 'The telephone wires

connecting people. They hum. When you're up close, you can hear them.'

'So?' I queried.

'So Ruth was joining in. Connecting herself up you might say.'

I would have hesitated to confide in another man, but I felt I could trust Waddington. Trust him not to judge, not to be shocked, not to gossip.

I poured myself a whisky and joined him at the table.

'Ruth was very disturbed that day,' I told him. 'She was on the point of leaving me. She was going to join her lover. The snow stopped her. She'd hesitated a long time, it seems. This was her last chance. He'd given her an ultimatum.'

'Yes,' said Waddington. 'I know all that.'

I took a deep breath. 'But perhaps you don't know,' I said, 'about Ruth's addiction to love. To falling in love. To unrequited love. From the beginning of our marriage it was happening. About six months after our marriage was the first time.'

'Actually,' Waddington said slowly, 'I did know that too.'

I have to say that at this point I felt somewhat peeved. I had the uncomfortable feeling that Waddington had learnt more about my wife in an afternoon than I had in fifteen years. I was conscious of feeling threatened — both personally, as Ruth's husband, and professionally.

'You see, it took me some time to talk her away from the pylon,' Waddington said, 'and even longer to walk her across the fields.'

'You walked across the fields with her ....? Well then ...?'

'Yes. You're wondering why I didn't bring her home.'

'I am,' I said rather coldly. 'Particularly as you'd obviously found her in a state of distress. Praying to a pylon hardly constitutes a sound state of mind.'

'That depends,' said Waddington equably. He settled

more comfortably in his chair, stretched his legs out and allowed me to pour him a second shot of whisky.

'Communication,' he said. 'She was praying to the god of communications. Not much different to the messenger god of the Greeks or Romans really, is it?'

'You'll be telling me next about dreams and the collective unconscious,' I said. 'The gods living on in us.'

Waddington grinned and shrugged. 'Your field, not mine,' he said. 'All I know about is animals. The primitive stuff if you like.'

I studied him carefully and decided he was playing the 'I'm just a simple man' game, under cover of which was considerable astute complexity.

'The snow has strange effects,' he continued. 'And that particular pylon, up high there and with the lines stretching across the landscape is ... well, dramatic. Almost everything else seemed buried under the snow.'

He leant forward, his elbows on the table, looking me in the eye. 'That afternoon it was a bit as if time itself had been blanked out.'

Waddington's close stare made me uncomfortable. I turned away. 'Well,' I said, 'If you're telling me that Ruth was praying to Mercury or Hermes — the messenger god — then I suppose you're trying to tell me she was mad enough to be trying to communicate with her lover, with Jim Forster — all normal means of communication being impossible.'

'No,' said Waddington. 'She was trying to communicate with you.'

I remember then that there was a sudden silence in the kitchen and that a shiver ran up my spine and that I thought, 'I don't want to know any more'. Waddington was watching me carefully.

'I took her back to the surgery,' he said. 'She was chilled to the bone and her boots were leaking. I dried her out, best I could. Gave her coffee and brandy. Then she talked.'

'I see,' I said.

'I don't think you do,' said Waddington. 'Not really. Ruth didn't want to go off with Jim Forster — or any of the others for that matter. If she did, she'd have done it long ago.'

'You're about to tell me what she did want,' I said as drily as I could.

Waddington was not abashed.

'Yes, I think I am,' he said. 'Ruth wanted you. But you were unreachable.'

'This is preposterous,' I said. 'I was home! I was home all day. You know as well as I do the village was cut off. There was no way I could get to work. I was home. Waiting for her. Worrying about her.'

'No,' said Waddington. 'I didn't mean reachable in that way. I mean she couldn't reach your heart. What she said was, "I can't find his lonely place. I'm shut out."'

'Shut out?' I repeated.

'Know your Shakespeare?' asked Waddington.

'We've had messenger gods,' I said. 'So why not Shakespeare?'

'That line,' said Waddington, '"Make me a willow cabin at your gate, and call upon my soul within the house." I think in a way, that's what Ruth was doing when she prayed to the pylon. She was calling upon *your* soul within the house.'

'And I didn't answer,' I said. 'I didn't send out any telepathic vibes or whatever. I think this is utterly ridiculous and, if you don't mind my saying so, quite offensive.'

'The yearning for romantic love,' said Waddington slowly, as if I hadn't spoken, 'is a kind of folly. And yet …'

'And yet?' I queried.

'And yet,' Waddington continued, 'it is a part of some intuitive knowledge about the capacity of the soul for love. A kind of hint of the divine if you like. Some days I suspect that when we cease to yearn for the great love of a lifetime, something in us has died.... but there, that must be the whisky speaking. I'm a plain man. Animals are my business.'

'You're suggesting,' I said, 'that this need was so large to Ruth that she couldn't live without it.'

'Couldn't make do like the rest of us,' said Waddington, downing the last of his whisky. 'You see I tried to persuade her about making do. I used some of the arguments I think you've used. She was more reasonable that you might expect. Said that all she wanted was to feel, now and again, that you'd touched ...'

'Touched?'

'Well...met. I can't remember her exact words. Something about knowing the bare human being. You know how she was. Flowery, at times.'

'A foolish romanticism,' I said.

'You could call it so. But you see I did bring her back that afternoon. I left her at the door. I'd talked for a long time about things like working at a marriage. How long it really took to get to know another human being. All that kind of stuff. You're probably better at it than I.'

(I thought this was sly of Waddington).

'And she said?' I queried.

'She said — she said she'd try. But then as I turned away — and she made me go — she said, 'But you don't know the man. He has ice in his heart.'

'That was all?'

'Her last words.'

'And you left her there? On the doorstep?'

Waddington nodded.

'Thank you for telling me,' I said.

Waddington stood up and we shook hands. 'I thought you should know,' he said.

'Yes,' I said. 'In some ways I'm grateful to you.'

As you might imagine, I sat for a long time that night finishing the whisky.

I thought of how Ruth must have looked in the window and seen me at my desk. How apparent it must have been to her that I wasn't concerned enough to come looking for her. To reach her, as she might have put it. She must have looked for some time. Regretted what she had said to Waddington about trying again. Could not bear to come in the house again. Better stone cold death than slow suffocation. She would have turned away and walked back.

I remembered how soon after dusk the snow had started to fall again. Remembered how she had been found. Almost as if she had made a nest for herself beside the tree, one of the farmers had said. And in a way, I now saw that was what she had done.

Was it any comfort to know that she had never planned to join Jim Forster? Some, I suppose. An ironic sort of comfort. For you see if anyone could have reached me, if anyone could have melted that ice in my heart, it would have been Ruth.

The truth is I have wanted the ice. Have cultivated it. Encouraged it to grow. Have preferred its coldness to the terror — the exposure — that is love.

Both of us, you might say, Ruth and I, have died of the cold.

◆ The Spare Room ◆

Iᴛ's ᴄʜʀɪsᴛᴍᴀs ᴀɴᴅ ᴀʟʟ the relations have come and therefore Hetty must sleep in the spare room. The spare room is a terrible, unlived-in room. Pieces of furniture, shrouded in dust sheets, camp there like refugees — a double bed, a chest of drawers, an anonymous armchair.

The only life the spare room has ever known is that of a bird which had flown in one day when the room was briefly being aired by some assiduous cleaner who had then, without seeing the bird, closed the window. Months later the trapped bird was found dead on the pale, untrodden rug.

'When a bird dies in a room,' says Mags (friend and confidante of Hetty's oldest sister, Rosa) 'it means that a murderer will come.'

Mags is a dramatic girl. She has a rich, deep voice quite out of proportion to her petite person, and she has just learnt how to throb it and throw it into mournful corners. 'When a bird dies,' she repeats, perched on the hearth in her party frock and practising the throb, 'that's what it means.'

Hetty knows she is making it up because Mags is enjoying herself so much. Nevertheless, she feels as if Mags accidentally has stumbled on some old mythological truth.

Hetty feels very cold. The fire is lit, the Christmas tree decorated. Her mother is chopping dark life into the pale boiled onions, adding sage to their watery skins. Rosa, newly married arrives with her sailor/husband. It's as if Rosa has become a stranger now and she and the sailor/husband are given the guest room with its new post-war finery — a silk bedspread and an eiderdown stitched into lumpy roses.

Aunt Lily arrives too. There is a family legend about Aunt Lily losing her soul when she was twenty and staying in her room for a whole year. But she has found it again now, Hetty observes, for she is an ordinary woman with a loud laugh and plump arms and she dresses in a way that Hetty's father calls vulgar. Hetty keeps an eye on Aunt Lily in case, like Persephone, she might just slip off to the Underworld for another stint.

Grandfather comes late, tipsy as usual from too much Guinness and with him Hetty's little fire-baked grandma, shrivelled up by insurances and penny-pinching and saying, as she says every year, that this Christmas will be her last.

All the fires are going now — in the sitting room and the dining room and the kitchen's Aga is working overtime. The turkey, in its basting dish, sweats like grandfather's forehead. Grandma, tucked close to the fire, seems turned into earthenware by henna and nicotine. Aunt Lily's eyes are as velvet as the new velvet curtains. The table is laid with the first crackers since the war. They are made of bright red crepe paper with gold doilies wrapped round their middles. Now and again Mags's dark voice throbs across the table all rough at the edges like a sword just drawn out of the stone and not yet honed for use.

Hetty cannot admit she is afraid. Downstairs, in the body of the house, eating turkey, popping crackers, she can see the silliness of Mags's story about the bird and the murderer. The bird in the spare room had been shovelled up and put in the dustbin by Hetty's mother, its eyes still wide open. Hetty's mother has taken away all the dust sheets in the spare room. She has put Hetty's own patchwork quilt on the bed and her old dolls.

Hetty's mother is pleased when she sees her youngest in the big spare room bed. Seeing her there, with her night-time pigtails and pink cardigan, is enough to bring the room to life for Hetty's mother. But not for Hetty. Hetty feels she hasn't enough life of her own to sustain this room, to give it all the life and energy it somehow seems to demand.

This room is separated from all the other bedrooms of the house by a long corridor. It is an L-shaped house, the L tacked on as an afterthought, a stray bit of story that the author wants as a kind of flourish, but which doesn't truly belong. Hetty wishes that the room underneath was occupied so that some warmth from the living might rise up through the floor boards and keep her alive. But the room below is also 'spare', though technically occupied by a ping-pong table. Hetty has tried and failed to turn it into a playroom. These rooms of the L of the house are unwarmable. Who knows about rooms really?

Hetty hears the familiar sounds of the evening — her mother bolting the front door, her father on the stairs, a last laugh from Aunt Lily, the flush of the lavatory, whispers (husky) from Mags, the small finality of the light switch click.

In her own room Hetty has ways of dealing with the dark. The Lord's prayer recited twenty times without mistake works like a charm. And there is the bedroom light of the house opposite to watch and its owner's silhouette to follow.

Here, in the spare room, there is only the sound of the big tree hustling against the window pane and not one, but two doors to watch. There seems no reason why the spare room has two doors — one leading out to the bathroom, the other to the hall. Perhaps the builder had in mind two rooms and changed his mind, or was thinking of the convenience of the weak-bladdered.

Hetty lies in the dead centre of the big bed that grows

bigger and bigger and she lies there watching first the left door, then the right door as if held transfixed by some nightmare tennis match. She is waiting for the slow turning of a door knob. She is thinking about the bird and how long it took to die and with what blind panic it would have hurled itself at window, door, ceiling. She is thinking about Aunt Lily's lost soul and Mags's murderer.

The door handle doesn't turn of course. And Hetty is lulled to sleep by her nightmare watch of door knobs. She dreams of birds for whom the sky is like a ceiling that traps them and Aunt Lily shut in her room for a whole year.

In the morning the grandparents leave and Hetty gets her own room back. But it is not the same. *She* is not the same. It is a new Hetty who sleeps in her own bed the next night while something of the old Hetty stays, like the bird, locked in the spare room.

◆ The Kiss ◆

MAGGIE PRYOR WENT on holiday to Crete prepared
and protected: body and soul. Her sponge bag contained sun tan oil in any number of factors, paracetamol,
anti-histamine, TCP, pills for diarrhoea and/or constipation, plasters, a plug-in anti-mosquito device. No condoms,
opposed as she was to the cheap souvenirs, the tacky airport
art, the Shirley Valentine clichés of holiday romances.

Maggie packed a modest swim suit, her long light skirts,
a Greek phrase book, and *The Odyssey* (pocket edition).
She packed her past. She packed (in her head) lists enti-
tled 'Achievements so Far', 'Securities', 'Career Plans'. She
packed her English self, all tidy and ordered, neat as the
patchwork fields and gardens of England over which she
flew to the Radiant Isle, prepared, prepared for everything
except light and love.

How could she have known, poor woman, taking every
precaution, locking up the house of herself with Yale and
deadlock, bolt and shutter, about that forgotten and un-
closeable window which, however small, gives undefend-
ed access to the heart? Or how guessed, that the sport of
the Gods that year was to linger over Iraklion Airport, in
search of a tourist to tease? There was Zeus, resting nude-
ly and languidly on a rare cloud (affronted by Maggie's
opaque self-possession), dispatching Hermes with a message to Aphrodite, goddess of desire, still bobbing about in
her shell (the sort used as an ashtray) on the Aegean.

Maggie should have had herself immunised — as for
hepatitis A B C and D — against the sea (given an ex-
tra-dazzling sheen by Aphrodite); against the lucid light

(fanned by Hermes' winged feet and calculated to get through the murk of anyone's psyche); against the sun (which melted thought and stripped off her skirts); against white crocheted linen (which prompted romantic longings); against lilies, geraniums and the occasional whitewashed loaf of a church (which ditto); against blueness (in which her personal past dissolved and the ancient one took over); against a dramatic congruence of sea and mountain (which churned up her passions) and against the unexpected kiss of Jack Morrison.

It was the kiss that finally laid Maggie Pryor open without getting her laid for despite all the efforts of the gods, Maggie had gamely hung on to herself, baring neither breast nor heart though all around her seemed to be engaged in one or other occupation.

Maggie Pryor, sitting on the veranda of the taverna where the vines tied themselves in love-knots and geraniums, scarlet as lipstick, shot and frolicked out of Knossos pots, reminded herself of how, like alcohol, sea, sun and sand broke down inhibitions. And was wary.

And when, in her bare white room (with only a lizard flittering in and out of the lavatory) the sea hushed and the moon stared and Greek voices ran and rambled like the vines, she told herself that this budding interest in Jack Morrison — in particular in Jack Morrison's hands — was just the standard Holiday Fantasy tape switched on by the unoriginal subconscious. Maggie even managed to laugh at herself and to feel a faint pride in what she regarded as her sensitive vulnerability to the spirit of place.

But all this was early in the week, before sea, lilies, blueness etcetera had fully worked their spell. And before the kiss.

It was one of those healthy alternative holidays. Maggie

did yoga in the morning and Tai Chi in the late afternoon. In between she swam, sunbathed, read *The Odyssey*, met up with others in the group to drink retsina on the taverna's balcony and compare lotus postures and to watch Jack Morrison.

On the very first meeting with Jack Morrison, Maggie decided that he was unequivocally not her sort of man. That there was absolutely no possibility of any kind of relationship with him was a great relief. Maggie sat back, enjoyed his company and, fatally, relaxed.

Jack Morrison was a short, balding, red-faced Cockney oil rigger. He told jokes. He made lists of new words he liked. He had the widest smile Maggie had ever seen on a man. He had a slow, predatory prowl. He would appear, at tee-total yogic suppers, swinging a rebellious bottle of wine between two fingers. He bought vulgar post-cards. He was both macho and vulnerable. He had square, short-fingered, slightly chubby golden-haired hands. Quite unspectacular hands but with a tenderness about them that held Maggie mesmerised. Whenever (as one of the group) she sat beside him, and his hand — with its shivering of golden hair — rested on the table, she was hard put not to reach out and take this tender paw in her own.

Jack Morrison, his prowl and his smile and his hands, sank like the sun into Maggie's being — each equally warming and hypnotic so that Maggie remained blissfully unaware (as indeed the gods intended) of what was happening to her.

And then came the kiss. It was the last night of the holiday. The group gathered at the taverna. They had been drinking Metaxu. Two earnest women talked of yoga and enlightenment. Unenlightened, Maggie sat on until there was only she and Jack left.

They stood up to say goodnight, Maggie still tidy, still self-possessed — though Aphrodite, doing her best, threw moonlight on her gold silk shirt — and Jack, warmer than ever on the brandy.

So he kissed her.

It was a direct, unpremeditated smacker.

'Sorry, sorry, sorry!' he muttered and prowled off into the darkness, head down like a bear.

The kiss spoke to Maggie's condition the way a book is said to do when you come upon it at an appropriate time in your life. The kiss cut through the layers and accumulated layers of Maggie's consciousness, right down, you might say, to the Minoan heart of her. No other kiss had quite reached Maggie-essence as this kiss of the tender-handed Jack Morrison.

And by morning — after a night when the whiteness of the sheets, the starryness of the sky and the sound of the sea through Maggie's open door, had combined to ravish her, it was all too late. Jack Morrison had taken an early ferry to Athens. Maggie bused to the airport where the gods were rewarded by the sight of a Maggie dispossessed of heart and reason.

Aphrodite put in a brief appeal for a more romantic denouement or, at the very least, a consummation of lust, but Zeus had little affection for tourists and in any case, having pledged a year's fidelity to Hera (to atone for dangling her by her gold-braceleted ankles out of the heavens) had even less concern than usual for the sexual satisfaction of mere mortals. And so Hermes was not sent (as Aphrodite wished) to snatch Jack Morrison from the ferry and hurtle him in an eleventh hour dash of suddenly-realised passion, to the airport.

Jack Morrison sailed happily away for ever and ever amen and Maggie flew weeping home to her tidy house and her tidy life and all of it, as she opened the front door, appalled her.

She unpacked everything but the kiss which rubbed and scrubbed in her heart like a pearl in an oyster, making itself at home, growing.

She upended her bag into the linen basket. The movement, like shedding an old self, made her look about to see what else could be shed, peeled away, thrown off. And then in a sudden access of almost hysterical energy she began turning out drawers, tossing out old clothes, ditching ornaments, hurling batches of letters into a box, tearing up career plans and financial schemes, throwing the antihistamine, the pills for diarrhoea and/or constipation, the TCP into the dustbin and finally and rashly unhooking the heavy sitting-room curtains and dropping them on the floor as if to make more light, more ancient light in which to live lightly.

Had she the energy, she might well have dumped the furniture out on the pavement but fortunately the journey had tired her out.

Even so, for several weeks Maggie cancelled all social engagements, neglected to update her c.v., padded about her now somewhat barer house in a limbo of obsession. (And all the while the kiss fattened and shone).

But slowly, as her tan faded, so the memory of sea and blueness faded and the obsession — with nothing to feed on — paled to an anecdote and the ancient light folded itself back into *The Odyssey* and Maggie took up her poor and personal past and was restored to her securities, her career plans, her ordered, successful, satisfying life.

Only on some evenings, drawing the re-hung curtains,

did she find herself going through her address book searching for a potential lover.

It was a safe enough occupation. None would possess
the kiss.

◆ Mozart in Heaven ◆

IT WAS OBVIOUS FROM the sky-blue radiance of the carriage where it had come from. And should anyone doubt, a neon sign on its roof flashed *HEAVEN*. During the night it parked itself outside Number 5 Belmont Street and there it waited, glowing and humming.

Lewis Porter, out late clubbing, saw it on his way home and thought at first he was hallucinating but then reminding himself that he had drunk nothing more than two bottles of Becks and a diet coke, decided it was a publicity stunt for 'Heavenly Veggieburgers', newly opened in town. What made Lewis smile was that this radiant carriage should have chosen to park itself outside the home of Misery Joe, Praise-be Joe, Hallelujah Joe and Mahatma Joe — known collectively as The Holy Joes. It was a good story to tell his mates at work, thought Lewis and he began rehearsing it. 'Imagine it,' he'd say, 'Misery will cast off his sandwich board. Praise-be and Hallelujah will be down on their knees and Mahatma will disappear in a neon flash of enlightenment.'

The Holy Joes had lived together for the last ten years. They were too holy to live with anyone else. Their ardour and virtue depressed people. They were undisturbed by the arrival of the carriage because they slept at the back of the house — Mahatma on the floor, Hallelujah in a narrow bunk, Misery on a bed of nails somewhat blunted by continual use and Praise-be on a well-sprung, Sleep-Easy Slumberdown mattress because he was the only one who thought it unnecessary to chastise the flesh.

On the contrary, Praise-be thought the flesh was something to be celebrated. He could be seen out in the back garden early every morning, whatever the weather, thanking God for the various parts of himself, beginning with arms, legs, eyes and ears and working systematically through all the organs of the body. It took him a month, was a biology lesson in itself and concluded with the wondrous cleansing power of kidneys and bowels.

At about the same hour, Mahatma would be sitting in the lotus posture meditating on a candle flame, trying to extend the warmth of his compassion to the peoples of the world, beginning with Birmingham.

All four of them had long ago ceased arguing about their religious differences. They lived ecumenically and none of them, for instance, ever mentioned that they wished Misery would repent of his Repentance and perhaps update the message on his sandwich board — one side of which read *Repent, the Kingdom of Heaven is nigh* and the other *The Wages of Sin is Death*. Even Hallelujah, whose evangelical preaching in the parks and gardens of the city had brought a thousand happy souls to Jesus, had given up on Misery. It was obvious to all that Misery's profound sense of sin was his purpose in life and that without it he would be utterly lost.

Praise-be (once Father Harris but now unfrocked and inclined to praise the Lord with some rather bad poetry and some excellent Chablis) was the first to see the carriage. It was the morning for lungs, veins and arteries and then time to reward himself with the purchase of croissants from the corner bakers and *The Sun*. Praise-be regularly declared that it was more important to be of *this* world than to be considering the next.

The carriage gave a small bounce as Praise-be opened the front door of Number 5. It hummed a little louder and its neon sign flashed more wildly. A feeling of unutterable horror sank Praise-be's heart to his sandals, but at least he had the wit to fall on his knees and sing out 'O Praise be the Lord! Praise be the Lord!' so loudly that Hallelujah, Misery and Mahatma all came to the door fearing that Praise-be was about to pay for his more gastronomic celebration of the flesh with a heart attack. Which, in a manner of speaking, it was.

'Brothers!' said Hallelujah, going into instant evangelic mode and voice, 'Our prayers have been answered!' And his face grew radiant.

'Christian prayers,' said Mahatma. 'Heaven is not in our vocabulary.'

As if in answer to this, the neon sign paled, wavered and in a few seconds became *ENLIGHTENMENT/REINCARNATION.*

'A trick! A spoof!' said Mahatma, but as he spoke the door of the carriage slid open and an angel with a clipboard in his hand stepped out. They knew he was an angel because of his abundant golden curls and the notches on his shoulders (rather like tin epaulettes) which were clearly where wings would be fixed when he was wearing them.

Misery began to weep. He seized Hallelujah's hand, dashing it with his tears. 'Farewell, dear friend, farewell,' he said and turning to the angel, 'Forgive me Lord, who am not worthy, whose multitudinous sins weigh down this soul with...' But the angel waved an impatient hand, turned over a page on his clip-board (solid gold, Praise-be noticed) and began reading out the names. All four of them were on it.

Praise-be was on his feet again now. 'If you wouldn't mind,' he said to the angel, speaking rather slowly and loudly as to a foreigner unable to understand English, 'I think I'll give this one a miss. I don't feel at all ready, you see. And frankly I think I'm more use down here than up there.' But the angel made a gesture with his hand and the four of them found themselves drawn towards the carriage like sleepwalkers.

Inside the seats were a plush purple velvet and the walls were hung with tapestries representing heaven in all its many guises and cultures. The angel was not to be seen, having taken the pilot's seat in the carriage's front compartment.

'I shouldn't be here,' moaned Misery, sinking into the purple velvet cushions that automatically snugged into every lump and bump of him which, due to his long stint on the bed of nails, were rather numerous.

None of the others responded. Praise-be was despondently searching his pockets, his mind running through a shopping list of things he would have liked to take with him — the silver-framed photo of his mother, his crucifix and rosary, his poems and the letters from Maeve...

Mahatma resisting the plush velvet cushions, sat on the floor in lotus posture and tried to focus his mind on the tapestry depicting the Buddha under a tree. It was almost impossible to stop the rush of creatures — potential reincarnations of Mahatma himself — who galloped, crawled, leapt, swam, dangled and flew through his mind. Please let me not return as an insect or a new-born child, Mahatma was praying.

Hallelujah's first flush of ecstasy see-sawed madly as he thought a) how wonderful it was that the Lord had sent His carriage; b) how sad it was that he would miss the Sunday service that would have allowed him to tell the evangelicals of this momentous experience. In his head he began to compose the sermon he might have given about the ways of the Lord in the twenty-first century. 'Expect His taxi every hour of every day. The meter ticks for every man. Go with hope but without luggage.' And so on.

Misery, still in his pyjamas, buttoned up his jacket and pulled the draw-string of his trousers tight. He felt ashamed and exposed. They were not even very clean pyjamas. Misery hunched his knees up to his chest. He had no doubt that once Praise-be, Hallelujah and Mahatma had been received Above, he, Misery, would be taken Below and in the foolishness of pyjamas when his choice would have been sackcloth and ashes.

A small window into the front cabin of the carriage allowed them to see just the golden top of the angel's head. The rest of the carriage was windowless. They were not to see the world they were departing from but they could hear a great roaring and beating noise which all of them recognised as the rush of wings.

Within the passenger compartment a light came on giving an instruction. *SETTLE YOUR MINDS AND SOULS* they read.

The Holy Joes looked at each other rather shyly.

'It's not easy is it?' said Praise-be. 'Being transported like this is — well, rather *un*settling.' Praise-be tried to speak as respectfully as possible, in case the angel could hear. 'Do you think our Friend in front could give us something that might help?'

'What d'you have in mind?' asked Mahatma, his level of compassion at low ebb, 'Milk and honey? Or morphine?'

'Breakfast might be nice,' said Misery and got an acute attack of giggles.

'O God, he's hysterical,' said Hallelujah.

At which moment the cabin door slid open and in came a cherub with a silver tray of what looked very like champagne. Champagne in glasses of such fineness that just to ping one with your little finger — as the cherub did (setting one before each of them) made a sound like the chime of a distantly tinkling planet. Praise-be relaxed. He began to think that if Heaven was as luxurious as the accoutrements of the carriage suggested, it might suit him very well indeed. This feeling deepened as he took his first sip of champagne and simultaneously heard piped Mozart. It was either the Kyrie Eleison from the *Requiem* or a new composition. Much as the drink tasted like champagne — or possibly Bucks Fizz — there was an otherness about it, an added tang that soon put them all to sleep, temporarily that is, until they landed.

*

They did not see the Pilot Angel again. The cherub swung open the carriage door and handed them each a boarding pass.

'What's this for?' asked Hallelujah, but the cherub put his/her finger over his/her lips to indicate that he/she couldn't speak.

'It says *Return*,' said Praise-be.

'To that other place,' said Misery beginning to tremble.

'No,' said Praise-be. 'It clearly says Return-Earth. Come on! This is the greatest privilege ever given to man. It's what everyone has always wanted to know. What comes after. If there's a heaven and what it's like. We can change the face of the universe when we get back!' And so saying Praise-be leapt from the carriage and found himself briefly floating in the ether before he dropped, light-footed as a cat, onto the floor of heaven.

'That rather depends on what *form* we come back in,' said Mahatma, following rather more cautiously. 'A spider couldn't change anything.'

Hallelujah had to hold Misery's hand and yank him out of the carriage. At first Misery refused to open his eyes but stood, a meadow of daisies tickling his bare feet, while the trembles were warmed out of him. When he did open his eyes Misery saw that there was a welcoming party for each of them.

Misery heard Praise-be's alarmed voice saying, 'We should try to stick together,' before a robe was draped around him and he was borne aloft on the shoulders of sixteen angels.

'And the last shall be first,' muttered Praise-be before he was carried off in something resembling a rickshaw by a troupe of junior angels with perfect bodies and a septet of cherub musicians playing so divinely and effortlessly that Praise-be felt himself swoon with pleasure.

Hallelujah was given not so much a welcoming party as a congregation of a thousand Souls. They were delicate, flimsy creatures, prone to giggle, to nestling together, to falling asleep. They provided him with a grand platform, a lectern (with a book that looked like a Bible but proved to be full of blank pages) and an attendant cherub who brought him iced drinks and chocolate truffles.

For the first time ever, Hallelujah found himself at a loss for words. He thought of suggesting a hymn and the cherub, as if reading his mind, immediately came forward with a clapper board that said *Dance no. 201*. The Souls immediately leapt to their feet and danced. They danced in circles and pairs. In circles and lines and solos. They danced dreamily. Frenetically. Swingingly. Then at a clap from the clapper board they dropped wherever they found themselves and turned their pale, attentive faces to Hallelujah.

Hallelujah found himself driven to telling them about life on earth, a kind of wide ranging current affairs programme that included his mother, his sister, the school at the bottom of the road, the situation in Syria, the scientist planning to clone people, the mad American president and the blue hyacinth he'd had for Christmas. Never had Hallelujah had such a rapt congregation.

Perfect peace was given to Mahatma by those who bore him away, took him to a temple, dressed him in saffron robes and laid him tenderly on a rug. Mahatma heard light bells, cymbals, distant chanting. It soothed him into a state of oblivion, nothingness, emptiness and then his mind flew from his body, across Heaven so that he saw Hallelujah with his congregation, Misery-me being baptised in the waters of eternal forgiveness; Praise-be receiving a massage to music for harp, flute and piccolo. Music clearly by Mozart. Mozart in heaven.

None of them was prepared for the return of the angel and none of them was quite the man he was when he arrived.

Praise-be had to be carried into the carriage by six rather hefty cherubs, his mind utterly stunned by music, his senses overwhelmed by beauty and luxury.

Mahatma galloped into the carriage like a loping and unsteady foal for during his out-of-the-body experience he had gone through several reincarnations — none of them as insect or new-born child. But the changes, from pig to tree, from lily to donkey, had happened at the speed of light so that although back in his own body, Mahatma did not quite feel inside himself and in fact his walk was never the same.

Hallelujah was steady but speechless. Misery-me, wild-eyed and full of energy, could hardly get into the carriage quickly enough being eager only to return to that profound sense of sin that gave him his identity.

The angel saw them on board, unclipped his wings, folded them neatly and hung them on a handy laurel tree for his return. The neon sign flashed *EARTH*, the cherub closed the door and they were off.

This time there was a kind of tea (though obviously laced and soporific) and the music sounded distinctly like Radio 2, though apart from Hallelujah, none of them seemed in any state to know or care.

Back at 5 Belmont Street, life — earth life — slowly resumed some of its old shape, but at root all was changed. Praise-be abandoned all luxuries (including his mattress) and the morning celebration of his physical parts. He gave up poetry and instead became obsessed by the flute which he played night and day until taken off to a psychiatric hospital where his Mozartian melodies made the other patients smile.

Misery-me could hardly wait to put on his sandwich board and although the message had changed, it was still not exactly to the others' liking. Misery-me's sandwich board (to the puzzlement of all in town) now read *The Wages of Sin is a Fearful Bliss.*

Mahatma returned to his meditational practice but in a more circumscribed kind of way, developing — despite himself — a fascination for both insects and babies.

Hallelujah was the most changed out of the four of them becoming wholly a man of the world. Hereafter known as Hector, Hallelujah married within two weeks of his return from heaven, had seven children and became a heart surgeon. He never preached again. 'A man of few words' was how Hector/Hallelujah was described and, by his devoted and loving patients, as 'very down to earth'.

◆ Somebody Smith ◆

THE THING IS, I'VE ALWAYS WANTED to be rescued. So when this young man comes to the door, all polite and nicely dressed and that, and he says 'I've come to do the rescue,' well, I go with him don't I? He shows me an official looking card but I can't read it because I haven't got my specs on. I think to myself there must be an emergency of some sort — *a gas leak perhaps or maybe an unexploded bomb somewhere.* And yes, I do think of terrorists but they seem very unlikely in our village, even if that's exactly what terrorists are — the least likely of folk.

Anyway, I'm not even in the village. Just outside it. There's only me and Mrs Parker — she's just down the lane, eighty seven if she's a day and I wonder if we're going to rescue her too, but it seems not, because I've hardly fetched my hat and coat (handy on the peg in the porch) when the young man — his name's Charlie — is hurrying me down the path, wanting to know if I've got my papers.

I've no idea what he's talking about so I just tap the side of my head and say 'It's all right, I've got it all in here.' Charlie looks quite impressed at that. And it's true what I said. I do have it all in here, in my head. My whole past. All seventy two years of it. Everything I've ever wanted to be rescued from.

You're wondering what, I suppose. Well, let's start with mother. Everyone wants to be rescued from their mother don't they? Mine was of the dampening variety. Life was just something to be got through by mother and you'd best just stay at home and let it wash over you. And then there was that office job — total drudgery that was. I used to sit over my typewriter tapping out invoice after invoice for J.M. Smallhearts Ltd wishing the typewriter would turn into Sparky's magic piano or something.

I suppose Jimmy rescued me from that in a way, marrying me when we found I was expecting. But very soon I was wishing someone would rescue me from Jimmy and rescue Jimmy from the drink only nothing and no-one did. Unless you count death of course.

I reckon I've been a maiden in distress and a matron in distress and now I'm an old lady in distress — but I'm never in quite *enough* distress, if you know what I mean. I'm always waving and never drowning.

And mostly, of course, I've wanted to be rescued from myself — me and my putting-up-with-it and do-as-you're-told ways. (That's mother again. Her instructions). So when things go wrong — I mean little things, like now, me being lonely and bored and the arthritis nibbling at me — I say to myself, *Martha Dryer, you should do something about it. Take charge of your own destiny.* But I don't, do I?

I just think about rescue. I think someone might knock on my door and tell me I've won a million pounds. Or a letter might arrive from some relative I never even knew I had, inviting me to China or America.

Mrs Parker's travelled a lot. I know because I sometimes pop in on her to see she's all right and usually when she's off in the kitchen making me a cup of tea I hear her talking to herself — she does a lot of that poor thing, she's losing it really — anyway, it was Russian or Greek or something. And she's got lots of books on her shelf, atlases, and dictionaries and books about politics and economics and such like. Once upon a time I suppose she must have been one of those what-d'you-call-em, intellectuals.

Anyway, the nice young man — Charlie — eases me

into the car and it's a really posh one, all leather seats and that and very soon my bum's quite warm so there must be heating inside the seat and I'd really be enjoying myself if Charlie wasn't going so fast. I'm not used to fast. Well, I'm not used to cars really. Sometimes I bike into the village but that's not so easy these days.

We're going so fast I daren't really speak and ask any questions like what's the rush and what's the emergency and is he going back for Mrs Parker because her place is a bit hidden down the lane and maybe he doesn't know about her and I wouldn't want her blown up or gassed or anything.

For myself, I don't think I'd mind going up in a kind of BOOM. I read a poem once by a lady poet — Somebody Smith — with a line that went *Come, Death and carry me away*. It stuck in my head that. *Come, Death and carry me away*. It sounds so nice and gentle, as if death had wings like a big soft bird. I sometimes think of it in bed at night when I'm not sleeping too well for the arthritis and I think it would be better to go quick and not get anything slow and nasty or lose my marbles like I think Mrs Parker is. Well, maybe not her marbles. Just her memory.

I sit very still in the car. I feel like holding on to my hat, but I know that would be daft. Charlie can't be more than twenty one. He's got quite a baby-face. He's a very clean young man. I think his mother must have ironed his shirt for him this morning because it looks very crisp. And his hair looks newly washed. He takes a pride, you can tell. I like to see that in a young man.

I shut my eyes for a while because of the speed and I tell myself that this is what being rescued is like. This is how it should be. Whisk and whoosh and off you go. Everything left behind. And I start to wonder if the house will still be there when I get back and then I think I don't really want to go back. That I'm thoroughly miserable there with no-one to talk to and Andrew — that's my boy - visiting twice a year out of duty and cleaning things no-one but me will see and watching the telly night after night. And then I think it's not enough to be rescued from something and that I want to be rescued *to* something else. A new life. A new me even, and I start thinking who I'll be, second time round, so to speak. *It's never too late*, that was one of father's maxims. Mother's was *what's the point?* And there never was a point, or not one you could explain.

I find I'm giggling a bit to myself and that's because I'm thinking how mother always told me never to get in a car with a strange man. And here I am doing just that at seventy two. A bit late in the day, but not *doing what I'm told.*

Charlie hears me giggling. 'You're a cool one', he says. 'But we're looking after you, don't you worry.' And he pats my knee, quite affectionately, as if I was his granny. I wouldn't mind being Charlie's granny.

And after that I nod off. It's the warmth under my bum and the speed and Charlie saying I'm going to be looked after. Next thing I know we're at an airport and suddenly I come round, as if I've been in a bit of a dream, telling myself that if you're being rescued you can't be too fussy about how it's done or where you're taken. But another part of me is thinking, *hold on there, how about a bit of choice? Human rights*, I'm thinking and I've never felt I had many of those.

Charlie must have seen me looking alarmed because he says again, 'We're going to look after you.' So I straighten my hat and I follow Charlie into the airport. And this airport is like a whole big city. There's moving stairs and pavements. There's shops and cafés and coffee bars. And gates. Umpteen gates leading to other countries and people queing up to go there. And maybe people who've been refused because they're sitting round looking miserable.

I follow Charlie up the moving stairs and onto the moving pavement and he's hurrying, hurrying and I can't keep up and anyway I haven't enough puff left to ask any questions or to say *Stop, Charlie! Wait for me!* I'm going off the idea of being his granny.

At last we arrive in this huge lounge, like it's a hotel and there's people sipping drinks and talking on telephones and all of them looking as if they're trying to be nonchalant and worldly only they don't really feel it. There's something tense, even about the men lolling on sofas in fine suits and shiny shoes.

Charlie leads me towards some men sitting at a table in the corner. There's three of them. One big, one a kind of dumpling and a stringy fellow with a beard. They all stand up when I arrive. Dumpling gives a little bow and shakes my hand. He's wearing dark glasses, though it's not exactly sunny in here. 'We're all very grateful to you,' he says, 'for what you've done over the years.'

'It's nothing,' I say, because that feels like the right response and after all, I have done a lot over the years. I've endured, that's what.

'We've got everything here you need Mrs Parker,' Dumpling says. And he's handing me a passport and a ticket and a brown envelope with what feels like money inside and I open my mouth to say *But I'm not Mrs. Parker!* And I close it again, quick, because the stringy fellow with the beard is looking at me oddly and he says, 'She don't look like her picture.' And all three of them turn to Charlie who's gone very, very pale.

And so many thoughts are flashing through my head I can hardly keep up with them. I'm remembering something I heard on the news about MI5 looking for an elderly woman who'd worked as a Russian spy for years and years. I'm seeing all those dictionaries and atlases on Mrs Parker's book shelf. I'm hearing her talk to herself in the kitchen. And I'm thinking — *I've got to rescue myself!*

'I think this is not she,' says the bearded one again. So I laugh a little and adjust my hat and say, 'Well, I've had to change my appearance quite a few times in this job.' And I carry on, I say, 'But I've had no info about this move' - I'm really pleased with *info* — 'there's papers in the car I must fetch.'

Dumpling turns all dark and angry at this. 'Go with her, Charlie,' he says, 'and get her back here fast. The flight leaves in under an hour.'

Charlie's looking pea-green by now, but I give him a wink and we rush off. At least Charlie rushes and I go as fast as I can.

Once in the car I throw my hat in the back seat and say, 'I'm not Mrs Parker. Drive!'

And Charlie drives, like the proverbial bat out of hell and when I look back at the airport building, I see Dumpling shaking his fist at the window and at that Charlie and I both burst out laughing and Charlie says, 'You're cool! Really cool!' I try not to smirk. I just say airily, 'Yes, but not Mrs Parker.'

So this is how it came about that Charlie and I rescued Mrs Parker — Naomi, as I call her now — from MI5. Because she'd be no use to them with her memory all in pieces would she? And there's no point in punishing someone for what they can't remember is there?

After a couple of weeks in a very pleasant boarding house, found by Charlie, Naomi and I moved into a very nice retirement home complete with warden should you need one.

So I was rescued in a way, from myself and from my old life. More importantly, I think I've found my destiny. It's not to be rescued, it's to be the one *who does the rescuing.*

After Mrs Parker, Charlie was the one I rescued next. 'Look, Charlie', I said, 'What's a nice young fellow like you getting mixed up with that lot for?' And Charlie blushed — he's still young enough to do that — and looked rather shamefaced and said he'd thought it would be exciting.

'They're just using you as a gofer,' I said. 'You should go-for something else.' So he did. Charlie works at one of these new health and sports centres now, he's what's called a fitness instructor.

Lots of people in the retirement home need rescuing — from grief or loneliness or wonky memories. I'm kept really busy. I said to the Warden, 'You should put me on the payroll', I said. But she only laughed. That makes a change, mostly she looks really sad. There's probably some rescuing to do there.

Must go. Here's waving at you.

◆ Somebody Palmer ◆

WHEN I WOKE UP I WAS IN this small room, possibly a cell. Nothing in it but a bed, a bedside cabinet and a wash-basin with a single tap and water coming from it. Cold water flowing from a tap. *Miraculous!* I thought, turning it on and off a few times. It was this and not any great white light that gave me the warning. Not the water from the tap, but thinking it miraculous. Which of course it is. A major feat of civil engineering, of civilisation, water from a tap, but you can't afford to be thinking so every moment when all you want is to clean your teeth or take a drink. A sense of wonder slows things up.

Anyway, it was by the miraculous water that I knew Christ was about to pay me a visit in my small room/cell. Not in person, you understand, the window being too small, but as The Holy Ghost which is as good as.

I sat on the edge of my bed wondering what to do and thinking how perverse it was of JC to choose this moment of my life to make an appearance. I had, after all, exchanged a god-fearing youth for a god-forsaken middle age, i.e. a modern man, miserable but modern. I felt aggrieved. And interrupted. I've had the odd numinous nudge over the years, something like the twinge of an old wound, but this, this alarming sense of immanence, felt like the whole Holy Ghost works.

At that point I thought I heard a voice saying *I do the forsaking around here*, at which I hid under the bedclothes and thought about rescue and about my brother Robert who, in the past, has rescued me from women, debt, alcohol and philosophy.

Maybe even now Robert was on his way, driving through the city streets in his old blue and white Triumph Herald. It would need to be a Triumphant Herald for this job. And then I thought that possibly The Holy Ghost might also be a triumphant herald, even if disguised as a puff of smoke. (How difficult it is to get away from these childish images!) Anyway, looking through the window there was no sight of an entrance or a driveway, only a narrow path and overgrown bushes, so I knew that as far as brother Robert was concerned, I was beyond finding.

I wondered if I was in prison or maybe on holiday (holy day?) in a somewhat sub-standard country hotel. I could see one or two people being led along the narrow path. This made me wonder if I had inadvertently stumbled into a home for the blind. And then I thought I was doing altogether too much wondering again.

Except ye see signs and wonders ye will not believe said the voice of THG.

I knew then that escape was my only option. I dressed as quickly as I could in the clothes I found there. I can't say I recognised them — an odd combination of a rather flamboyant shirt and a cheap suit that might have been worn by a salesman — but I presumed they were mine because they fitted. Quite apart from the miraculous water and the terrifying prospect of signs and wonder, I was getting intimations of goodness. No, not goodness, virtue. They are not the same. Often enough, I've tried goodness — sending a present to a child, a cheque to Oxfam, phoning a friend in need, listening to same. Little bits of goodness, you might say, mixed in with the general sweep of things. But unlike virtue, goodness carries within it a suggestion of niceness, a quality I have always thought dubious. You can hear a smirk in the very word niceness that implies the desire to be liked or admired, for niceness truly wishes to be liked or admired.

But this, this that I felt wafting towards me was altogether different. Not exactly sainthood, you understand, because in my aforementioned god-fearing days (when the hunger and thirst was upon me and I might have hankered for signs and wonders) I quite fancied sainthood — provided no martyrdom was involved — and pictured myself drifting, St Francis-like, around the woodlands talking to the birds and the gentle foals and deer and being fed by the Hand Of, or perhaps on berries. Looking rather ascetic but not feeling the cold. That was another delusion Robert rescued me from.

No, this was virtue of a different order. I knew that at any moment my room/cell was going to fill with light. An unbearable, transforming, radioactive light that would go right through me and then it would be goodbye lovely mortal sin, the indulgences of the flesh, the appetites, the senses. The crème fraiche, the plush seat in the concert hall. All gone. This was no longer caring for appearances. The fine suit, the soft shoe, the silk shirt. I mourned them already. And how I would stand out in any crowd! Not in the manner I prefer to stand out, when standing out is what I wish, which happens from time to time — i.e. immaculately dressed, cultured, wise — no, none of that — but poor, powerless and radiating virtue, driven, at all times, to speak up, speak out.

And then there was adultery. No more of that. Indeed no more lust, infatuation, the romantic adventuring without which life would become incurably drab. It was this last that propelled me to the door, dressed now and remembering Somebody Palmer.

Clothed and in his right mind, said THS. It sounded more

like a question than a statement. I didn't wait for more. A memory had returned to me that I had met Somebody Palmer in this building and that we had sat close together, our backs against the wall, comforting each other with a little sensual frisson. At least I had been comforting Somebody Palmer and had been comforting myself in the act. I thought that if I could find her now I would leap into bed with her and we would snuggle together beneath the blankets, sinful and safe from the blinding light.

Blinding? Of course it would be so. Something like lightening. Or should that be lightning? Possibly both. This could be the explanation for the people I had seen being led down the narrow path. I could be living on some ley line or fault line that gave THG access.

So out of my small room/cell I go in search of Somebody Palmer, only to find there's a guard dog outside. She's sat up high at a desk wearing a badge that says 'Sister Lopez'. There's a small lamp on the desk that throws a greenish light on Sister Lopez's face. It's a deeply furrowed face as if Sister Lopez has known trials beyond belief. They have not made her kindly.

Sister Lopez points a finger at me. 'Back to your bed,' she says. Odd how even at my advanced years I respond to the voice of authority, retreating like a child. On reflection, and sitting down on my bed again, I am not sure if Sister Lopez said 'back to your bed' or 'I shall silence you with my syringe'. Possibly both.

But now I have a dilemma, for it is perfectly clear that Sister Lopez is not a woman to be charmed by a story. Nor do I think she possesses an imagination. Were I to tell her about the immanence of The Holy Ghost, she would think I was mad and might well lock me up. Also, even before

His/Its arrival, I know it is beholden on me, not to tell. 'Beholden'. It is not a word I am comfortable with.

I am between Sister Lopez and The Holy Ghost. Or between the dark of one and the light of the other and of the two, the light is the greater threat. I have no option but to try again.

And this time I'm in luck because Sister Lopez has left her desk. There is someone in the far distance, wailing. Someone who is probably in for the syringe. I close my door behind me. I have it in mind that Somebody Palmer was living on the floor above mine. At least she was when I last saw her, for it's come back to me that she wanted to die and was thinking of ways of doing it. Indeed had tried to slit her wrists with a broken dinner plate, only unfortunately the plate was of such thickness that it provided no cutting edge.

All of this made me hurry. Up a flight of stairs. Along a corridor. And another and another. The place was awash with men in white coats. I thought I could have been The Holy Ghost himself, so little notice did they take of me, or of anyone else for that matter. They had the mastery of the pre-occupied look and the brisk walk that might equally well be en route for a cup of tea or major surgery.

Anyway, I was grateful not to be noticed and for myself I tried to cultivate a walk and expression that implied I knew where I was going. I am reasonably well practised at this having the need, now and again, to use the lavatories in various institutions like the university or the offices of LRT Inc and have found that a purposeful stride and an avoidance of eye contact with doormen and the like, is almost infallible.

I was listening for the sound of female voices, or for the

smell of. I came upon a wall poster advertising the hours of a hairdresser and felt I must be near. I began to worry that Somebody Palmer might have found the means, other than a broken plate, to do herself in before she and I could unite in saving sinfulness. To give myself some credit, I was prepared to settle for a cuddle on the grounds that a lustful thought would be as great a deterrent to THG as the lusty deed.

I had just spotted a woman in a rag of a dressing gown going, zombie-like, into a room on the left in which I glimpsed a number of other women seated round a table apparently making clay pots, when I saw two men marching towards me, one in a white coat, the other in black.

It was the black and whiteness that got me. Not the coats alone, but the sudden overwhelming notion that the world was black and white, good and bad and that there was no place for the grey of myself. I do myself an injustice. Not merely grey — there are purples and dark blues in there and sometimes a dash of beach yellow.

Whatever. I cowered in the corner beneath the hairdresser's jolly poster and the two men, one in white and one in black, took an arm each and half led, half dragged me back down the stairs.'Palmer!' I shouted, 'Somebody Palmer!' And I was dimly aware of a woman leaning over the stairwell and looking down at me. She threw me a flower, a tulip I recall, scarlet and with its petals opening wide as tulips do in the beauty of their death throes. I clutched it as if it were grace itself before White coat and Black coat thrust me back into my small room/cell while Sister Lopez, arms folded over her bosom, watched with satisfied approval.

But all was not lost, for within a few minutes a young woman followed me into the room. I don't think it was Somebody Palmer because this woman was young and alive-oh with bouncing fair hair she must have washed that very morning and breasts adequate for both man and child, but I could be wrong. Perhaps she'd heard me calling her. Perhaps I'd suffered the briefest flash of virtue and this, though it had done nothing to me, had transformed Palmer into a woman with a vibrant desire for life. At any rate I heard Sister Lopez instructing her to stay with me but on no account to talk.

It must have been late afternoon because I immediately observed, with relief, that my room/cell had darkened to the extent that the tulip I was still clutching was vibratingly scarlet. It was bright enough to serve as a bedside light.

At once I tried the tap. Good, ordinary water flowed out of it. I cupped some in my hand. Drank. I filled the tumbler with the wonderful ordinary water and stuck the tulip in it. Then I slept. I don't think I felt the syringe.

◆ Mrs McCoy and Moses ◆

B EING BETWEEN LUSTS and mellow fruitfulness, Mrs
McCoy had decided upon a day of piety. Or rather a
day of piety had decided upon her, for Mrs McCoy's chol-
ers came and went as they so pleased and she suffered their
arrival and departure as best she could.

Either she was a woman of infinite variety, or she was
possessed by the cast of the Royal Shakespeare Company,
or else her nature was akin to a computer that plays its one
programme *ad nauseam*. Who can hazard at the truth?
But Mrs McCoy favoured the last of these theories on the
grounds that whoever she was, she was not herself. In the
main she felt like one who has studied meteorology for de-
cades and is still unable to predict the morrow's mood of
rain, hail, sun or storm.

So did this day of piety catch her without her umbrella,
so to speak, when with a moment's retrospect it would appear easy enough to have predicted it.

The vicar had been to call. Now although he was an ungod-
ly man, fond of a liberal use of the Anglo-Saxon, still some
incense-odour lingered about his person. He had brought
her a book about Thomas Merton and Nowness. And then,
as if it were a signal for Mistress Piety to begin her speech,
the picture of Moses, coloured by Mrs McCoy's daughter,
unsellotaped itself from the window pane, slid through the
slit in the radiator and lay in sin upon the floor.

Apart from all this, Mrs McCoy was fair sated with love,
sex, death and poetry and it was a Monday, the washing
machine broken and the weather of unmitigated greyness.
Mrs McCoy's computer program was limited to the afore-

mentioned topics plus God. This observed, it should have been a matter of great simplicity to predict a day of piety.

She would have liked to wallow in the guilt of her meteorological failure but piety would allow no such indulgence. Mrs McCoy set to, contemplating first Moses, then the breakfast dishes, then Nowness.

Clearly Moses could not be left on the floor. Mrs McCoy picked him up and studied him. The portrait had been made on tracing paper so that when coloured and sellotaped on glass, produced, if poorly, the effect of a stained glass window. Moses, courtesy of Mrs McCoy's daughter, had a red and blue war helmet, a purple robe, a yellow face (scrolls to match) and bright green eyes. Under his nose was a kind of doctor's mask, inexplicable to Mrs M.'s daughter who did not know that Moses's face to face encounter with God had left his own phyzog so shining, so aglow, that he had had to hide it from the common multitude. A little of Moses's beard protruded from under the mask. He had been on the window about a year. A grey oblong (and four sellotape marks that would be tedious remove) bore witness to that.

Mrs McCoy found herself full of jealous hatred for Moses and resentful of his veil. Why, having had such a rare privilege, did he keep it all to himself? What harm would a quick shufti at glory do to anyone? What were the Israelites afraid of? One look might have melted their software and selved them holy. She was tempted to crumple Moses into the bin but wished to do so with indifference. Angry blasphemy was only next door to faith. Mrs McCoy was not stupid.

She put Moses down and began on the dishes and Nowness.

They were of comparable difficulty, there being several

burnt pans and each Now as unholdable as water. She had to continually yank herself back from time past and time future into time now — if there was such a thing, which she began to doubt.

As for the pans — Mrs McCoy reminded herself of a lover who had once been given a quantity of such pans to scour and had survived the occasion by chanting 'The Buddha is in the pot! The Buddha is in the pot!' Mrs Mc-Coy tried it. But the phrase evolved, as phrases will, and became 'Sod God'.

Though it lacked originality, Mrs McCoy was pleased with it. Indeed she thought about leaving the pots and tele-phoning X who, she was sure, would enjoy 'Sod God', for only last week he had advised her that for the sake of her health she should say 'Fuck the Pope' three times a day.

However, such was the piety upon her that she decided not to telephone. Instead, the dishes finished, she stood, broom in hand, mind travelling the length, depth, breadth and cobwebbed height of this domicile which, due to her formal upbringing, required that she clean and tidy it.

It was a gloomy prospect and she shied at it but Chris-tian valour was at her heels that day and telling herself that eternity was in a grain of dust, she began to sweep the floor, wondering all the while why, if she were to live in the Now, she could not be given a more interesting Now to live in? (She bore, it will be apparent, a great grudge against the mysterious ways of Our Lord and refused altogether to traffic with Christ, finding his descent to earth lacking propriety.) Mrs McCoy was stolid Old Testament, liking the virility of an angry, jealous God, one with a penchant for drought, famine, fire, flood and pestilence — all mat-ters which she felt to be proper for a God. Gentle Jesus lacked machismo.

Finding it impossible to nail any thought to the Now, Mrs McCoy began talking aloud, itemising the possessions about her. For some minutes this proved an interesting occupation.

There, on the shelf, were old blue and brown bottles salvaged from the dump by Mrs McCoy's husband, Tom. Was she not fortunate to have a husband who raided the inarticulate and brought forth blue Milk of Magnesias, brown Schweppes, one delightful ink bottle labelled 'Field's Ink and Gum' — all now numinous with age? On the dresser was a mug with a rainbow handle given to her by X. It was rare indeed to find a love who possessed soul and sexuality in more-or-less equal degrees. In fact, as she looked about her, it came upon her that this room was peopled (by way of teapots, jugs, pots and mangles) by a positive horde of friends and relations. Nowness had revealed it to her. Here she was, balking at the duster, blind to the animate symbols of love and of history.

But the sop and sentimentality of this 'count your blessings' attitude only sufficed to put her in a passion. So what? she cried. So what? (Give the woman her due, her contempt for Christ was equalled by her contempt for false comforts. She was a proud bitch and it is possible that the Great Jehovah intended to give her the Job-treatment so that she grovelled for any comfort.)

However, she fought Him gamely. In her younger days she had aspired to such profanity as would cause Him to strike her dead. Maturity had taught her that no amount of abuse would provoke the Bastard. That determined, she decided that no platitudes about Nowness would reduce her to doing the housework with sweetness and joy. She was not, in fact, prepared to do it at all. Dung and death, dust and decay. What was the point? (She lacked the humour to suffer futility gladly).

Piety, however, was not yet defeated. It delivered The Sermon on the Mount, recalled to mind various paths of enlightenment, reminded her that she must go by the way wherein there is no ecstasy and concluded with a homily on moderation and the still centre of the turning world where is the dance.

All this was somewhat wasted on Mrs McCoy, but then God was an Infinite Wastrel. Mrs McCoy knew well enough that moderation and the middle path was the Right Royal Way but it was impossible for her to take it. She had no middle to her nature. She was programmed to alternate longings for ecstasy or oblivion.

And therefore Mrs McCoy prayed to God to cast her into the darkest pit so that from there she might try to sing. (The logic of this is hard to find and there is probably no more to it than that it was more interesting to sit, with coffee, cigarettes and anger, contemplating the possibility of pure joyous song springing from purgatory than it was to wield the broom).

God being indisposed as usual, Mrs McCoy took to Eliot's *Four Quartets* as a substitute for her craving. Now although she had read these before, on that particular day they spoke to her condition — as the Quakers will have it. In particular she was hauled ashore by the lines about waiting without hope, love, faith or thought. Such positive negation had her enraptured. She found it an immense relief to abandon all four, pronto.

She memorised the lines, lay on the sofa and listened without love, hope, faith or thought to the Brandenburg concertos (which suffered as a consequence) while quietness and peace invaded her various zones.

It was all a cod of course. Piety had won the day and cast its spell upon her so that Mrs McCoy quite forgot the thousand and one times she had hung her life, like her coat, on the peg of man, beast, poem or philosophy.

She had fought and lost and therefore now lay in a sort of deluded trance (which was possibly necessary for her physical survival) believing that she had now truly found the answer to life and was prepared to wait, simply wait, gallantly and for a lifetime.

In the event she lasted three days during which time she went about with an air of serenity admirable to behold. She also wrote to most of her friends telling them that she had no wish to see any of them at the moment as she was waiting without etcetera etcetera — an action she was soon to regret.

Her insincerity might have been detected from the fact that Moses remained where he was, neither on the window nor in the bin, neither in the to nor in the fro.

The cause for Mrs McCoy's lapse from piety is of course inexplicable. Either her computer programme moved on or else the peg, the frail branch on which she had hung her tonnage, snapped. Whatever the cause, Mrs McCoy grew tired of waiting. Explosively tired. She wanted action. Love, sex, poetry or death action. Any action. Futile action.

At which point in the Now she opened up shop again and cast her myopic orbs on that small portion of the universe given unto her.

Moses she took out of limbo and with fresh sellotape set him up again. There was nothing to be afraid of. An English sun illuminating a portrait of Moses would not be too blinding. And anyway, she'd lived with him for a year — or was it a lifetime? — and still found his bright green eyes irresistible.

♦ Confession ♦

THIS MORNING I DROWNED a spider in the kitchen sink. I know that in the hierarchy of sins, this is far from the worst. Indeed far from *my* worst. Still, I feel bad about it. Years ago, before I knew any better, I used to drown spiders without a pang. My children taught me kindness to spiders — and flies and bees and wasps. Also I learnt disposal methods. The piece of paper and glass method. Spider climbs onto paper, glass comes down and there he/she is in a little dome, ready to be carried out to the garden. Alternatively — and good for sinks and baths — a towel laid over the side lets him/her climb out and away.

This particular spider caught me by surprise. It was the first spider in my new house, my new kitchen and my new sink. I'd already turned on the tap when it started to crawl up the side. Towards me, as they do, and I panicked and just turned the tap on full.

Why does it take so long to drown a spider? I've never forgotten Beckett's story, *Dante and the Lobster*. Belacqua's aunt is about to cook a lobster.

'But it's not dead' protested Belacqua, *'you can't boil it like that.'*

Lobsters are always boiled alive, his aunt replies and Belacqua tries to console himself with the thought that it will be *'A quick death, God help us all.'*

But it isn't of course. Nor was the spider's. Wildly it ran every which way to get out of the reach of the jet of water. I just wanted its legs to disappear. I wanted it to become a black anonymous blob. A nothing. The plug hole of this new sink has very small holes. I thought the spider would never go down. And when it did, I had this absurd fantasy about it whizzing out the other end of the drain (wherever that is) and skedaddling away. Traumatised no doubt. But alive. Off to tell the other spiders about its terrifying ordeal.

I was trying to excuse myself, of course. I can remember an old flame saying, '*God loves a happy sinner*,' and my being wholly convinced of this. Of course He does, I thought to myself and I could imagine God smiling down on me in a rogueish kind of way. It was a good excuse for adultery, God smiling like that.

Listen, I wasn't brought up to care for spiders. I grew up in the era when flies were swatted and spiders flattened and we still had hanging.

You should know better.

I do. I just slipped up.

There is no excuse for murdering a spider.

I'm scared of them.

That's an excuse? People said that about harmless old women they thought were witches.

I know.

Actually, ever since the drowning episode (let's neutralise it) I've had this urgent need to confess. But somehow I think confession's indulgent. There are loads of people out there who've had it in for spiders. They'd understand. We could compare notes. I'd feel better. But no, I should bear the secret of it. I shouldn't even be *writing* about it.

And the Lord only knows why I'm making such a big deal of it. I mean sin is just totally out of fashion. It only exists as a kind of distant concept. What we have now is *feelings* that we need to become *aware of* and then we can *work through them* and become better people. It's all O.K. now. If I envy my neighbour it's because my self-esteem is low and I need to do something about it.

I miss sin. Original and unoriginal. I miss the drama of it. The suspense of wondering if I'll be redeemed. The forgiveness of my many trespasses. The hope of grace. Damn it, I miss the guilt. All my adult life I've loved the Catholic novelists — Mauriac, Greene, Spark, Flannery O'Connor. Not just loved. Envied! The grand drama of their *under the aspect of eternity* plots. I suppose the sin of envy would combine with the sin of hypocrisy if I turned Catholic just in order to become a Catholic novelist.

But clearly my psyche believes in sin, even if my intellect disputes it, because this morning, when the spider was at last nothing more than a black blob, its legs all drawn into its middle, I thought of its death being added to my list of sins and wondered how it would rank.

I still do this from time to time. Think about Judgement. Think about the accounts book where it's all written down. Debit and credit. Good deeds and bad, a kind of Continuous Assessment. For this process I think there may be an Australian kind of God. One who turns everything upside down so that what I think are my great achievements, my kindest acts, barely get a mention, whereas smiling at someone who looks lonely on a bus scores really high. This idea is comforting when your great achievements aren't that great and for the days when smiling at someone on a bus is the best you can do by way of loving your neighbour or anyone else.

It's *not* so comforting if you apply the same system to your bad deeds (never mind thoughts) because on this reckoning, drowning a spider would come out really high. On the whole, I think that unless there are marks for trying, I'm done for. I'm rattling on about this spider for several reasons, or probably as many reasons as a spider has legs. Here's two:

1. To make you think what a tender-hearted, compassionate creature I am to go through so much angst over a mere spider.

2. Because I'd like nothing better than to confess to all of the seven deadlies — wrath, envy, lust, gluttony, avarice and sloth. But

a) I'm too ashamed to do it, and

b) other people's confessions are so embarrassing.

In my teens I used to read a magazine called *True Confessions*. As far as I can recall, most of the confessions were to do with betrayals. In my twenties I moved on to sterner stuff. Unamuno's *The Tragic Sense of Life* and Kierkegaard's *Fear and Trembling* and *The Sickness Unto Death*. I doubt anyone has thought up such an outrageous title before or since.

Kierkegaard is hot on sin. '*Sin is this*,' he writes. '*Before God, or with the conception of God, to be in despair at not willing to be oneself, or in despair at willing to be oneself.*'

A kind of no-win situation really. Or a catch 22. I don't think I ever truly recovered from Kierkegaard, but I gave him up. Held on to despair instead. There! I've slipped it in. The biggie. The secret.

To get back to my record. It's possible that this includes a long list of flies, ants, bees, wasps, spiders and a variety of other insects all murdered by me in ways both fair and foul.

Ants, for instance. I've poured boiling water over ants. And I've put down that sticky stuff called *Nippon* that makes you think of Japanese prisoner of war camps. And that powder that you puff into all the cracks.

I've nothing really against ants, except that this particular tribe seemed to be eating their way through my concrete back doorstep. I think possibly they lived underneath it. I half expected the door step to lift up one day and a regiment of ants to march off with it borne on their shoulders. I read a book about ants once and was impressed by the way they run their communities. Also I like watching them. Watching the way they can balance tiny little stalks on their backs. The way they work. I just don't want them making off with my back door step.

It's the same thing people say about the homeless, or those being rehabilitated into the community, the mad and the bad — *We don't want them in our neighbourhood. Not on/under our doorstep.* All of it prompted by fear for family and property. By lack of charity. *And though I have the gift of prophecy, and understand all mysteries, and all knowledge; and though I have all faith, so that I could remove mountains, and have not charity, I am nothing.*

A lack of charity for all God's creatures is enough to make anyone despair. So that's a double sin, I suppose. I read a novel by Narayan recently in which the narrator describes how, as a child, one of his grand-uncles gave him a coin every morning so he could buy sugar for the ants. I felt as small as an ant when I read that. But then I reasoned that probably the ants weren't under the grand-uncle's doorstep and that 'various corners' of the house isn't the same as an anthill in/under said doorstep.

Anyway, I do have attacks of remorse about pouring a kettleful of boiling water over the ants. Several kettlefuls, actually. But who knows? Being scalded to death by boiling water coming out of the sky may be a quicker way to die than the powder that dusts them so that in all innocence they carry it on their backs to poison all their relatives in the anthill. Perhaps they get drunk on the sticky Nippon.

The point is that I can *justify* — to myself, if not to the Lord above — killing the ants. Even more so flies and wasps, both of which are a threat to health. Flies all look alike, don't they? They're also exceptionally stupid. I often try to help a fly escape by opening the window wide, turning off the light, flapping them in the right direction. Will they go? No. Centuries of evolution haven't taught flies to understand window panes. Their panic is worse than mine with the spider. If you ask me, they prefer to batter themselves into exhaustion against the glass. I've also sat by and done nothing when a fly or moth frizzles itself to death on a light bulb.

It's my experience that no two spiders look alike. They're solitary creatures. Individuals. Also useful. Remember that children's book, *Charlotte's Web*? And how Charlotte befriends Wilbur the pig? Before she dies (naturally and having giving birth to several baby spiders) Charlotte says to Wilbur, *A spider's life can't help being something of a mess, with all this trapping and eating flies. By helping you, perhaps I was trying to lift up my life a trifle. Heaven knows anyone's life can stand a little of that.*

Mine too. Not that I believe that one good deed cancels out a bad one. (How have I got to be so *mathematical, so commercial* about my sins?) But you have to admit that some good things come out of guilt. I don't know why therapists are so against it. For example, when I swim my twenty lengths of the public baths, it is an act of penance for smoking an equal (equal? Don't make me laugh! Double more like) number of cigarettes. If someone was to re-write the ten commandments right now, they'd add smoking. Slow suicide. Therefore despair. See how I'm slipping it in, in a sneaky, circumlocutory way?

This afternoon I told my neighbour about drowning the spider. I did it casually, so it didn't sound like a weighty confession. Or maybe I did it that way to avoid judgement.

He responded quite merrily, running up the steps to his flat and calling, 'It happens! It happens! We've all done it!'

I bet you if I'd described the spider's death to him, fully, in all its leggy, panicky scrabbling, he wouldn't have been so cheery about it. Probably wouldn't have let his little girl come into my garden ever again. Anyway, *We've all done it*, isn't any comfort. The thing I'm talking about here is shame. That feeling you get when you imagine everyone knowing your secret. People pointing at you in the street and saying, *There's that woman that drowns spiders and pours boiling water over ants.*

I know my shame about killing the spider won't last long. By tomorrow I'll have forgiven myself and resolved not to do it again. And I don't truly think I'll be a reject from heaven just because of a spider. No, it's rather the way shame accumulates over a lifetime, like barnacles on a shell. All the hidden shames. And the layers and layers of self-deception that make you blind to them at the time — the psychological damage you did to your kids; the neglect of your parents. Etc. Etc. Etc.

Oh all of it a lack of love that includes drowning a spider.

◆ The Lady of the Sea ◆

B ECAUSE THE CHILD WAS SO SMALL, the father had to place a cushion on the passenger seat for her. Every night, after their drive, he put the cushion carefully away as if it were somehow special or dangerous, like a gun. He put it on the top shelf of the gardening cupboard and tapped the door three times in a kind of code.

The mother complained about these evening drives in a wailing, ineffective way while she did the washing-up.

'She's not a boy,' she said, 'She doesn't like cars. And what's the point? Driving round and round in the dark… what's the point?'

Leo would let the question hang in the air. 'Well anyway,' he said, as if in the pause the dusk had made some answer, 'I'll take her down to the sea front — give her some sea air. It will help her sleep.'

Lucy was asthmatic. Leo and Martha talked of moving out of town, out of their narrow terrace to somewhere by the sea where Lucy could breathe properly. But it wanted money and Leo and Martha were more attached to the town than either liked to admit. The town gave them a framework, a known order. Out in the country they both felt secretly lost and clumsy.

'It's almost vulgar,' Martha had said once of the tall, richly flowered hedgerows of a Gloucestershire holiday. 'All this growing and flowering — like a woman with too much make-up.' Stone was what Martha liked, stone and mortar, brick and pavement, a feeling of being inside something, not exposed on a hillside, a target for the elements, an object to be swallowed up in a wood, or shrunk like Alice, by the vastness of fields. Within a town she was enclosed and safe. There was a sense of purpose about a town that comforted her.

Leo too belonged to the town but differently, irritably, as if he wished to shake it off but couldn't, like someone born into the wrong family who is permanently uneasy yet cannot bring himself to leave.

So it was that after dinner Leo would loosen his tie, undo his shirt button, crack his finger joints for a while, smoke his cigarette and then turning to Lucy say, 'How about a drive?'

And Lucy always nodded and ran, at once, for a coat or jersey, her pale, peaky face expressionless as she stood before her mother and allowed her to smooth her hair with a damp, dish-watery hand.

Sometimes they teased Lucy because she spoke so seldom.

'She's lost her voice again,' Martha would say over the dinner table.

'It's drowned in her eyes,' Leo replied.

It sometimes seemed to Martha and Leo that everything that was said sank in those eyes of Lucy's and drowned there. It made her almost a mute.

Lucy loved the car. She did not dare confess it. She knew they would take advantage of it, tease her, use it as a bribe, joke about it to their friends.

They went out into the dark garage. Leo was a bulky man and when he eased himself behind the wheel the leather seat creaked until he was accommodated. Lucy sat high on the small cushion feeling the snugness of the old Rover with its wooden dashboard, the dials and knobs ranged before her like a choice of journeys.

Leo liked to warm the car up slowly. He switched on

the ignition and set the first small lights to glow. Then the choke came out and he let the engine run until he could reduce the choke and have it purring nicely like a nervous animal soothed.

The cigarette lighter was a gadget that pleased them both. As the engine idled Leo pressed in the knob and they waited until it clicked out and he could draw it forth, glowing red and magical in the dark of the garage.

His cigarette lit, Leo eased the big car out of the garage, a tiger from its cage, and they were out on the road, the engine noise softened by the dark space around them so that they were more conscious of the rhythms of the tyres and the streets evolving out of the night and falling away behind them.

Lucy, silent as usual, fell into a sort of trance initiated by the motions of Leo's hand on the gear stick, the steady rock of the wheels, the padded wood and leather of the Rover and the darkness that gave a dimension of lunar spaciousness so that the two of them, close in silence, seemed to journey in no-man's land.

Leo drove out of town and through the tunnel that took them under the river to the other side of the estuary. The tunnel was hateful. The two lanes narrow and circumscribed, the roof low, the lights small and interrogating and set in ruthless regularity along the damp walls. It was like swimming under water for longer than you could hold your breath. And indeed they *were* under water. Above them was the grey and oily merchant water of the River Mersey. They drove under the very sea through this tunnel, murky despite the lights and with the walls slimy from condensation.

Then they were out! The road rose upwards, the two ticket booths loomed above them like the gates out of purgatory. Leo wound down Lucy's window and she reached out to give the man their tickets. 'Evening, missy,' he said, tipping his cap, and they were off again, faster now, with Leo humming and Lucy, her eyes momentarily bright, sitting up expectantly on the cushion eager for the sea.

There were no street lights now and the roads were wider, emptier, open to possibilities. Lucy could see the outlines of trees and behind them rough Wirral sandstone rocks with scrubby patches of gorse. Sometimes the headlamps caught the yellow gorse and made it blaze out of the darkness like the Burning Bush.

In ten minutes they reached Rinklake. It was not the most exciting of seaside places to take any child. Its atmosphere was one of decayed gentility. Tall Edwardian houses lined the promenade; the sea was railed behind respectable green railings. Here and there a bench or shelter had been set by the Council as though sea-watching was a spectator sport to be done with a thermos of tea.

Leo and Lucy didn't sit. They walked, Leo briskly with his chest flung back and his hands linked behind his back; Lucy at first sedately and then, as the noise of the sea pulsed into her, making her its echo chamber, she skipped and hopped, climbed aloft the railings and shrieked and shouted at the sea. No words. Just sounds.

Sometimes while they were there they heard the lifeboat maroon go off, a deep boom, as if from under the water, and a shudder went through Lucy's body as if she couldn't find within herself a sound to correspond with the depth of that boom, its toll.

When the tide was out they walked down the cobbled slipway where the shrimp and kipper boats rested and Lucy could run across the sand. This part of the Dee estuary was perfectly flat. Beyond the distant frill of the tide line was a nothingness inhabited by salt winds and shifting skies, a space, a something grand that Lucy dragged down into her asthmatic lungs like an addict of sea air.

At length Leo, looking at his watch, would catch her up. 'It's time,' he would say. 'Our lady will be waiting.'

Our lady lived at the far end of the promenade in the last of the Edwardian houses. Her living room was on the first floor and the front window had been made into a gazebo from which you could look out on the whole of the estuary as though you commanded the sea itself.

It was here, on these nights, that Lucy sat perfectly quiet, perfectly contented, a pale flush in her cheeks. To herself she played a game about the lady being the Lady of the Sea, telling the tides when to come and go. When the Lady died, she, Lucy, would be the next Lady of the Sea. Lucy clasped her hands in anticipation of this and listened to the boats moored out in the water, the halyards clinking against the masts like the sound of souls clinking in chains.

The lady herself looked, to Lucy as if she had come from the sea. She wore soft blues and greys but her eyes were a terribly fierce dark blue as if they had soaked too long in a foreign ocean and not yet faded to an English climate.

In the bathroom, the lady's bath was shaped like a shell and the brass taps formed the mouth of two fishes. Lucy had turned one, tentatively, but it spat, jetted and spat again so that Lucy hastily turned it off, suddenly afraid that these fish-taps with their Midas-gold lidded eyes, and their harshness under the hand, were the control taps of the sea.

The lady's voice attracted and repelled Lucy. There was a roughness to it like grains of sand gritting over pebbles and wearing them down. And her smile, to Lucy, was too brilliant. Yet it was right that the Lady of the Sea should be fearsome, that her eyes should terrify, her voice scrape, her bracelets clink like the boats moored on the water.

Lucy was content that she herself saw little of the lady. Once they had settled her in the gazebo, offering books, drinks, games — all of which Lucy refused — the lady and Leo went away to another room.

There, Lucy imagined, they talked of the tides, planned the weather, doomed half-a-dozen boats, saved another, decided to whom they would award a mermaid. She did not think about it too much. The whole mystery was too big for her. One day she would know. One day *she* would be the Lady of the Sea.

Eventually Leo returned to the front room and picked up his coat. The lady did not return. She remained elsewhere, perhaps controlling the oceans from her bath-like-a-shell.

'Come on, little one,' Leo said to Lucy and she too picked up her coat and they went out into the cold sea air that momentarily took you by the throat.

On the return drive Leo sang in a low baritone and occasionally glanced at himself in the driving mirror and stroked down his moustache, trim and still slightly blonde.

Lucy lay back in the soft leather of the Rover as pale and exhausted as if she had been rescued from a storm at sea. Yet happy. Happy with the deep peacefulness of an accomplished rite.

Lucy never mentioned the lady to her mother. There was no conscious deceit in this, it was to do with the tunnel. The tunnel beneath the river separated the town world from the sea world as successfully as if they had been two different planets or rather two different spheres of time.

And Martha didn't ask. When they came in her face was closed and pinched. She made them a cup of tea and turned on the television. Once she put her hands on Lucy's cheeks and said, 'I can feel the sea in them,' and shivered a little.

As the winter drew on the evening excursions became more difficult.

'The car is hardly a novelty now,' Martha said in a certain dry tone, 'And it won't improve Lucy's asthma to be taken out on an icy January night.'

Leo shrugged and put on his coat without looking at Lucy. 'All right, I'll leave her,' he said. 'But I need to go. It settles me at night to get away from the town. Gets the day off my back — like shedding a skin.' And he laughed lightly as though his journey were no more than a walk round the block with the dog.

He didn't return that night. Ice on the road, they said, black ice. He had come through the tunnel and on that lightless road, open to possibilities, the road where the yellow gorse blazed, he had skidded into a lorry. There was hardly a body to bury. Leo had shed his skin, and more.

Martha took the news almost as if it was all she could expect from life. Grief and bitterness fought within her and because she was a proud woman and wanted no comfort from anyone, it was the bitterness that won, outwardly at least.

But Lucy was hysterical. Terrible attacks of asthma left her whey-faced and hollow eyed. Often she hardly had breath to speak at all, but when she did it was always to rasp out the same words — 'He's gone to Our Lady,' she said. 'He's gone to Our Lady.'

Martha propped more pillows behind the child's back and yet again tried to hoover the room free of dust. She thought, bitterly, that she would be forced to leave the town for Lucy's sake and live elsewhere, probably by the sea.

She paid little attention to Lucy's words. The child had several Catholic friends up the street. One of them had given her a cheap Pieta, plastic and gaudy with a Walt-Disney-blue Mary and a disproportionate medieval Christ. Lucy had propped it up on her dressing table until Leo had seen it and thrown it away.

Even in a feverish sleep Lucy said the same thing over and over — 'He's gone to Our Lady. He's gone to Our Lady.' Sometimes Martha had to bite her lips to stop herself saying 'He hasn't gone to Our bleeding Lady! He's gone to the cemetery down Kington Lane — or what's left of him has.'

But denying comfort for herself, she yet wanted comfort for the child. What did it matter if the child wanted saints and angels? If it made her feel better why take them away? What was the point?

And so, a few days after the funeral, when Lucy again lay heaving for breath in the small town house, saying 'He's gone to Our Lady,' Martha knelt down beside her and stroked the child's brow and said, 'Yes, I expect he has. And Our Lady will look after him and love him and take care of him.'

And the child's taut chest relaxed a little. Her breathing eased and she slept.

✦ Just Breathing ✦

IT WAS ONLY WHILE SHE was ill and vulnerable that Nina thought about possession. About being possessed. If it really happened. And if it had happened to her.

Back home and convalescing from the asthma attack that had whisked her off to Lark Green hospital in the middle of the Easter holidays (why did illness never strike in term time?) Nina was able to rationalise it all. Talking to friends she described Madge as 'this old woman who took a real shine to me'.

But it had been more than a 'shine'. And what Nina never repeated to anyone was Madge's last words. 'I'm going. You've come to take over.' That's what Madge had said before her eyes went wide — with astonishment or terror, it was hard to tell — and a noise like someone gargling on phlegm came from her throat. Nina had pressed the buzzer for the nurse. Then there'd been curtains round Madge's bed, more awful gargling and the nurse apparently slapping Madge's hand and trying to call her back from the brink. 'Mrs Dawson! Mrs Dawson!' How odd, Nina had thought, to be called Mrs Anybody on one's death bed. Then there'd been a final terrible retching, as if Madge were coughing up her lungs and it was all over.

Or rather it was just beginning. Nina had gone back to her own bed and listened to the awful sounds coming from behind the curtains while Madge's last words bound her, like a petrifying kind of spell. A spell, Nina had thought, was not an instant thing, as it was often made out to be in fairy tales. Rather it was something that worked on you slowly and you didn't know it was happening until the final magic words were spoken and then it was too late.

Thinking about this now, in the study which was really Tom's but he allowed her a corner, and trying to prepare next term's school work — though her usual enthusiasm seemed entirely lacking — Nina told herself it was ridiculous to think of Madge casting a spell. She herself had been in a state of nervous shock. What with Tom not wanting to call the GP, then the ambulance in the middle of the night and the oxygen mask — just like the one her father had died under. Then the hospital itself and the nurses, sailing up and down the ward, their little white hats like paper boats on a river, casting rhetorical 'all rights?' to the left and right of them and not wanting to disturb the houseman. Nina spent the whole night heaving for breath and thinking she was going to die — not of asthma but of mortal carelessness; of the English dislike of making a fuss, shared apparently, by nurses, GPs and Tom. At a certain point in the night she had felt as if the world had shifted on its axis.

And then there had been Madge, lying there like a Government Health Warning personified. Nina was not a heavy smoker. Never more than ten a day. Not what you could call an addiction. And Nina didn't. To herself, to that part of herself that somehow remained rootedly Catholic, she called it a sin. To smoke was to commit slow suicide, therefore, ipso facto, it was to be guilty of the sin of despair. Had she still been in the habit of going to confession, this is what she would have confessed to. Despair. (Possibly not mentioning the fags). Nina liked the romantic flourish of 'sin of despair' compared to the flat metallic sound of 'addiction'. Psychology had done nothing for the language. Consider melancholia/depression. Listlessly, Nina turned the pages of the National Curriculum advice on English Literature.

No doubt it had been a combination of terror and residual Catholicism which, that night, had magnified Madge into a personification of the twentieth century's eighth deadly sin. Smoking. Propped up by a stack of pillows, all skin and bone, hair sweated to her head, two black pools for eyes, a green Ventolin inhaler fixed (with a permanent look) over her mouth, Madge had gazed out at Nina like a latter-day Cassandra. Indeed it had been Madge who had kept vigil over Nina all night. Madge who had pressed the buzzer for a nurse when Nina, too breathless to call out, had realised — and really it was the last despairing piece of carelessness — that her own bed was not fitted with this essential piece of patient equipment.

Nina abandoned the National Curriculum and went downstairs to make herself a cup of coffee. Not that coffee was worth having without a cigarette and she and Tom had quit. To quit. What a quick, cutting verb — onomatopoeic, in a way but wholly inappropriate for the long, shaky, gut-gnawing, hand-trembling process of giving up fags. The kitchen — indeed the whole house — felt curiously claustrophobic this morning. Nina was tempted to wonder if it was claustrophobia rather than fags that had prompted the asthma. Or was this yet another wriggling evasion of the addict's mind?

She nibbled an unpleasantly hard ginger biscuit and thought about Madge. It had been that first night, that vigil, that had bound them together, one breathless soul to another — Nina with her feeling of 'there but for the grace of God ....' and Madge? Nina tried to put herself in Madge's shoes. Or rather Madge's bed. In which (so she had learnt from the young gossipy nurse) Madge had been lying — and dying — for four months. January, February, March, April, literally and slowly passing away with the effort of just breathing. It was a stint of suffering long enough to test anyone's belief in a loving God. In four months He would become punishing. Or indifferent. An inexplicably slow sort of death, like Madge's, would drain away not only your health and strength, but any possible meaning life once might have had.

Nina took her coat from the back door peg. A walk, some fresh air was what she needed. There was nowhere really to walk except towards the park, up past a long row of shops that seemed to change every other week; charity shops and second hand clothes being the most long-lasting.

The thing was that her arrival in the ward had given Madge an explanation, given meaning to those long months of terrible endurance. You see what you feel, thought Nina, finding herself, automatically and seemingly without intent, in the tobacconist buying twenty Benson & Hedges. (Twenty!) She had felt guilt and therefore had seen Madge as a Government Health Warning. Madge, feeling godforsaken, had seen Nina as — as what? Daughter? Doppelganger? Beloved? Heir? 'I'm going. You've come to take over'. The one she had been waiting for — like in a relay race when you have to hand on the baton. The Lord had it all planned really. There was a reason for suffering. Or rather the human heart had to find one.

'I'm so glad you've come,' Madge had said, the next morning when, after a powerful injection of steroids (the doctor having put in an appearance at last) Nina was up and breathing and sitting by Madge's bed, holding her hand. And Nina had heard no more in this statement than ordinary politeness, something a hostess might say to a guest at a party — 'I'm so glad you've come' — not the unspoken 'at last'.

Nina paused at the corner by the park and lit up. A sweet giddiness overtook her. A month without nicotine and this was like her first ever Woodbine, bought illicitly in her teens, smoked with the gang, walking along the sea front on a Sunday evening after church. Ciggies, they were called then. Not fags. Nice friendly ciggies. How she and Madge had laughed about Woodbines. (Not that Madge *could* laugh, though you could tell from her eyes she was trying).

'Wild honeysuckle,' Nina had said. 'Imagine calling a cigarette that today!'

'More like cancer-suckle,' said Madge, which was brave, considering.

After Madge's death, Nina had wondered, briefly, if she should try to find out more about Madge's past. What she had inherited, as it were. Just who and what she was 'taking over' from. 'A woman of enormous emotional energy,' Nina said out loud, sitting down on a park bench under a dead elm and lighting a second Benson & Hedges. Because of course that was what had been so astonishing about Madge — the quality you could, well, love her for. Almost nothing of her left, physically, yet what you felt was this energy, this still passionate desire to love and be loved. Madge was not a woman who would stay stuck in a school for fifteen years trying to cram Eng. Lit. into reluctant ears. No. And nor would she stay claustrophobically married… Nina stamped out the cigarette. If she had learnt some *facts* about Madge's life, she wouldn't now be in danger of making her up. She could have asked the young couple who had visited Madge one evening. They'd stood silently at the end of Madge's bed as if they feared death might be infectious. Which of course you could say it was. The whole human race caught it. Madge herself seemed indifferent to their presence, feigning sleep, not attempting to remove her oxygen mask and talk. Nina saw the young couple looking at each other as if trying to decide how long a stay constituted a duty done.

Leaving the ward the girl had looked at Nina as if, after a silent half hour with Madge, she had to speak to someone. 'You wouldn't think she was a fine musician once would you?' she said. She had spoken bitterly as if it was all Madge's fault that she could no longer play whatever instrument it was she'd once played so finely. And maybe it was. All those friendly ciggies taking over from flute, clarinet, oboe, whatever. Perhaps the girl was a distant niece. It would have been possible to get her name and address from the nurse. But Nina hadn't. She hadn't wanted to know. Had been too frightened by then. Instead she'd gone off into her own memory of applying for a place at a music college and failing and having to abandon the dream…

By the fourth day in the ward, the 'thing' with Madge — Nina still preferred to call it this, the only alternative suggesting itself being 'a whirlwind love affair', which was somewhat ironic considering its short and static nature — had somehow got out of control. It had been like finding yourself the unwitting object of someone's passion, thought Nina walking moodily out of the park and back up the main road of shops.

But had she been unwitting? And why, try as she might to explain away the whole brief encounter as just the product of Madge's desperate, dying delusion, could she not do it? Instead she found herself facing that old and foolish question continually asked by the abandoned lover, 'did she really love me?' And there was no clear answer to this except that something had got so close to Nina's heart that it hurt. She'd been moved and repelled.

It had happened in the afternoon. Nina had been reading to Madge and Madge had fallen asleep. Nina was just about to go back to her own bed when Madge woke, pulled the mask away from her face and nodded towards the third patient in the ward. 'She's jealous of us,' she said. That was all. But it was grotesque. And grand.

The third patient was Mrs Doreen Biddle. Speechless and semi-paralysed after a stroke, the large grey lump of Mrs Biddle lay in bed with a plastic sack of urine hanging from her side. Every now and then, when Mrs Biddle scratched herself with her one working hand, the sack fell on the floor and then the nurse came and tutted and attached it to Mrs Biddle again and tucked it back in the bed, tidy as a miniature hot water bottle.

Most days Mr Biddle came and sat by Mrs Biddle's side and then her eyes spat with silent hate. 'It was all his fault,' the gossipy nurse explained to Nina, 'he left her on the floor all night.'

The idea that Mrs Biddle, preoccupied with hating her husband and no doubt desperate to know if she would ever recover the use of her limbs and larynx, had the emotional energy left to be jealous was preposterous. And the small gloating smile of power that accompanied Madge's words was shocking. And what, oh what could Mrs Biddle have to be jealous of? In one of those awful moments of recognition, Nina knew that answer. That even in extremis, paralysed, speechless or dying, the human heart hungers for love. For intimacy. Madge had claimed Nina as her own. And Nina had allowed it. How else explain the fact that she had never once crossed the ward and sat by Mrs Biddle's bed? Held Mrs Biddle's hand? Mrs Biddle had seemed to belong to another world.

Nina stopped outside the Violin Shop. She often stopped here. The window was appealing. A cello was set up on a plinth with a music stand in front of it and behind the cello hung a line of violins, shapely as nudes, their wooden torsos polished, the dark holes of their mouths saying 'O, O,

O. Play us! Play us!' Nina went in. She half expected to find the distant niece there, but she wasn't of course. It was a man in a brown apron, polishing a bow.

It had been unreasonable to be frightened of Madge's last words, to fear possession. So thought Nina now, walking down the line of violins and selecting three to try. Years since she'd played, but she hadn't lost her touch. The man in the brown apron looked quite impressed. In the hospital, still in a nervous state, she hadn't been able to see beyond Madge's death. The only thing she could see herself 'taking over' was the manner of Madge's death. As though she too was destined to spend four months gasping for breath, dying as slowly as a human being knew how to die. That was all nonsense of course.

Nina paid for the violin with her Access card. Tom would probably create, but it would be too late by then. She'd be gone. Off to seek whatever it was Madge was still seeking when she died. If she was taking over anything, it was surely Madge's energy.

Nina smoked half the Benson & Hedges with several glasses of pre-supper wine. Tom had shaken his head over it and then joined in. He'd been nice about the violin. Said he'd been thinking of buying her one for her birthday. This could be it.

'You seem like a new woman since you came out of hospital,' he said.

'Do I?' asked Nina. 'I feel quite like my old self.'

◆ The Medicine ◆

NOWADAYS MY TWO SISTERS don't speak to each other. They haven't spoken for years and years. They haven't spoken ever since the day Betty accused Rosa of feathering her own nest on what should have been family money and in response Rosa called Betty a traitor. Rosa's the oldest, Betty's next and I'm the go-between. Not that I've done much go-betweening of late. They're both too stubborn. Both unforgiving.

The reason I'm the go-between, even though I'm the youngest, is because there's only four years between Rosa and Betty but I was born a long time later. Twelve years later than Rosa, eight years later than Betty. I was either an after-thought or my parents' last attempt at having a son. One or the other. Anyway, so far *beneath* Rosa and Betty that I couldn't compete, couldn't be a rival. Well, a *rival* isn't quite right. It's more that I was too young to be the cause of jealousy.

But this isn't about nowadays, it's about back-then. Back when we were nearly a happy family — despite rivalries and jealousies. And it's about the night Betty nearly killed me with her looking-after.

I should tell you that I loved Betty and worshipped Rosa. Betty was the homely one. Rosa, the adventurer. Betty, in back-then-time, was the ugly duckling. Her hair frizzed. She had buck teeth. Acne. She could sing like a nightingale but my father thought she was dumb and packed her off to boarding school. All through term time I pined for Betty.

Rosa was tall, dark, dramatic and distant. She painted her nails and her mouth scarlet. Perhaps it was just because she was tall (which Betty and I weren't) but her life seemed to be lived on an altogether loftier plane. Even the bus she caught to the beauty salon where she worked was a double-decker and Rosa a top-deck person.

Rosa had boy-friends. Innumerable boy-friends. They came to call for her. Betty and I watched them through the banisters of the top landing. They looked well-washed and sheepish. Rosa treated them all the same. Superciliously.

Betty didn't have boyfriends. She went about the house singing *Some Day My Heart Will Awake*. I hoped it would. And soon.

Rosa — and Betty during the school holidays — took it in turn to babysit me. *Babysit! The indignity of it when you're eight and three-quarters!* This was because twice a week my parents went to the cinema. *The Flicks* as they called it. Every Tuesday they went to The Winter Gardens and again, on Saturday, because that's when the programme changed. Mother dressed up for it. From the bedroom window I'd see them going down the road, she on father's arm and looking ever so proud and both of them looking as if they didn't have any children at all, as if they were just boy and girl friend. It was quite outrageous the way she smiled up at him and he smiled down at her.

And after the cinema, on the way home — when I should have been asleep and wasn't — I'd hear them laughing together and, on a Saturday night, the rustle of paper. Then I know they'd been to the Chippie for six pennyworth. The way they joke and quarrel about the chips with mother giggling and pretending to keep them all to herself, would make you think they were the children. Then the garden gate gives its wooden bump and I'd know they're back being proper parents again. At least until next Tuesday.

Rosa's method of 'babysitting' and Betty's method are

very different. Betty lets me stay up late. She makes cocoa in a mug, stirs it all up nicely, and puts lots of sugar in. Then we sit in the kitchen and drink it together. After that she makes me a hot water bottle and snugs it in a towel. When it's time for the bathroom Betty sits on the loo and chats while I get washed and do my teeth and when I'm in my pyjamas she tucks me in, reads me a story and waits while I recite my lengthy prayers, blessing everyone I can possibly think of. Also, she makes sure to leave the landing light on.

Rosa's method is to get me to bed as soon as possible and with the minimum of attention. Have I washed? Cleaned my teeth? Who cares! And though usually I'd be quite pleased to forget both, I'm slightly hurt by this indifference.

Looking after me is so boring for Rosa that usually she asks her best friend round. Mags is petite and glamorous and though I don't recognise it at the time, she has a kind of French chic. She also has a wonderful voice — deep, throaty and amazingly large for her petite person.

I know perfectly well that Rosa and Mags are going to sit in a huddle and share beauty secrets and boyfriend secrets. For all I know they may smoke and drink. What I do know is that I'd give my eye teeth to be allowed to sit and listen but that I never am.

Time for bed, Rosa commands. Do I imagine it or is it even *earlier* than the hour named by mother? Even if it is, I daren't protest. It's amazing the authority height gives you.

So I go. It's terribly bleak and lonely. I miss the comforting cocoa. I hate the dark stairs. I have to fetch the bathroom stool and climb on it to switch on the landing light. The bathroom itself has turned chilly and the bed without a hot water bottle is cold. I strain my ears to hear Rosa and Mags talking but they've shut the living room door. I doubt they'd hear me if I was murdered in my bed by the bogey man who visits the spare-room on Tuesdays and Saturdays.

Nowadays — just to leave back-then to back then for a moment — I've forgiven Rosa all this because she got to like me more as I grew older and she stopped stinging my legs with nettles when I interrupted her reading in the garden and became a Mainstay and Support, defending me whenever I needed defending, which turned out to be quite often.

Also, I should confess, that even when Rosa was ignoring me or stinging my legs with nettles or threatening to cut off all my hair if I so much as opened the door of her bedroom — which I did, of course, because it was like a magic cave of dance dresses, beads, earrings, a whole beauty parlour of lipsticks, rouges, mascaras — that even then, I still worshipped her. And there was a small traitor in *my* heart because although I loved Betty, Betty of the loving kindness, it was Rosa I wanted to be when I grew up. I felt she had Destiny. She was going to ride out into the world on her double-decker. Off to Africa, or India or wherever there were grand adventures.

Was Betty jealous of Rosa? How could she not be? Rosa's looks. Rosa's boyfriends, Rosa's stature, Rosa's commanding confidence. And just a little later, Rosa winning the equivalent of the Handsome Prince and lots of money. At supper time, when they sat side by side, Rosa would poke a finger at Betty's spots which often grew red and ugly. *Yuk! Yuk! Yuk!* Rosa would say. Was it that, that hurt, which lay festering (as raw and ugly as the spot Rosa pointed at) for twenty, thirty years until Betty accused Rosa and Betty responded by calling her a traitor because Betty said she'd had enough of the belonging to the family business (and

Rosa's nest-feathering) and was going to sell all her shares. So there!

But back to Back-Then. Back to the night when Betty's loving kindness, Betty's looking-after nearly killed me.

It was winter, not far off Christmas, and I was poorly. I was prone to bronchitis. Mother said I had a weak chest and made me wear a liberty bodice. She laid her head against my chest and said she could hear the kittens in there. And I wheezed away so she could hear the little new born kittens crying. Bronchitis came regularly enough for no-one to worry too much about it and anyway the doctor said I would grow out of it. Mostly, when the worst of it was over, I enjoyed being poorly. Being allowed to stay in bed and read or come downstairs and curl up by the fire in father's chair with a rug round me.

I was on the mend that Tuesday night when Betty was the one left to look after me. She was not long home for the Christmas holidays. I think she got double babysitting duties when she was home to make up for the time when she wasn't. Mother was doubtful about going out at all but father said there was a Humphrey Bogart film — *The African Queen* — and he really didn't want to miss it.

'She'll be fine,' father said. Father had no truck with illness, he thought people got ill on purpose. *What d'you want to go and get a cold for?* he'd ask and there was no telling him that you hadn't done it deliberately. 'She's almost better,' father said. 'And Betty will look after her.'

Mother fussed about a bit. I knew she was reluctant to leave me. I also knew she'd go with father. She often had this conflict between us and him and father always won. Sometimes I thought father didn't really want children, or certainly not daughters. He'd prefer it if we were all sent off to boarding school. Forever. Then he and mother could be just boy and girl friend again.

Mother dressed up as usual in her smart coat and hat and court shoes. I was sitting up in bed. Mother made me put my pink cardigan on over my pyjamas and fasten all the buttons. She re-did my plaits though they didn't really need re-doing, plumped up my pillows and eiderdown and adjusted the curtains. She stroked my cheek and said I looked very pale. I thought she wasn't going to enjoy Humphrey Bogart's *African Queen* very much. Finally, mother showed Betty my bottle of medicine and instructed her to make sure I had it before I went to sleep.

The medicine was pink, like my cardigan. Pink and thick and gluey. It had a slightly sweet, dry taste. Mother put the bottle on a saucer with the spoon beside it. Betty promised not to forget.

Soon after mother and father had gone, we heard Rosa going out. She didn't bother to say goodnight to us. Betty let me hop out of bed so we could look out of the window and see who she was going out with. It was Johnny Drumond from the Young Farmers' Club. He was rather podgy and red faced. We saw Rosa slide very elegantly into his sports car. It was as red as her long finger nails. Betty pulled a face and drew the curtains again. I hopped back into bed. I didn't feel *very* ill, just what mother called *peaky* which I think was a combination word meaning pale and weak. I was glad it was Betty looking after me, not Rosa.

I didn't feel like cocoa, but mother had left some Lucozade so I drank a glass of that and Betty read me not one, but two stories, snuggled up beside me on the bed, just under the eiderdown. Then she said it was time for my medicine. She fetched the bottle and shook it up, just like mother did and read the label. I knew it off by heart. It said *One teaspoon four times a day.*

Ah, but then there was Betty's kind and loving heart. Betty read the label over and over as if she was thinking hard. And she shook the bottle up again. There was enough in it for another week.

'If you had more than one teaspoon you'd get better quicker,' Betty said. I couldn't dispute the logic of this even though deep down I thought it couldn't be quite right. After all, the instructions on the bottle came from the doctor. But what if the doctor wasn't as bright and intelligent as Betty and I?

And then I suppose Betty was overtaken by the ambition of her loving heart. What if she could make me better very *very very* quickly? Say overnight? Say by the time mother and father came home? (Not to mention Rosa).

Betty spooned the medicine out, teaspoon after teaspoon. After about six of them it became horribly sickly. It was like swallowing glue.

'That's a good girl', Betty kept saying over and over again. 'That's a good girl.' And I didn't want to upset her did I? I loved Betty. 'Make you better soon,' Betty crooned, at least it sounded like crooning, that thing mother said Bing Crosby did, because I was getting sleepier and sleepier and by the time we got to the bottom of the bottle I could hardly keep my eyes open.

And that's how Betty nearly killed me with her looking-after. At least that's what mother said when she came home, found the empty bottle of medicine, rushed up the stairs and shook me awake. Mother marched me round the bedroom and down the corridor and back again until I was dizzy. And sick. Because of course eventually I threw up all that pink gluey medicine in the bathroom basin.

Downstairs I could hear Betty weeping and saying 'I just wanted to make her better! I just wanted to make her better.' And father's answering, 'Dumb! Dumb! Dumb!'

Which Betty wasn't of course. She was wise of heart and sweet of voice and I forgave her for nearly killing me with the medicine just as I forgave Rosa for stinging my legs with nettles and packing me off to bed too early.

And nowadays I wish I could give my sisters some medicine of forgiveness. Something maybe pink and gluey that would make things better, make them start talking, glue them together again. But the best I can do is this story, which I recognise is a bit tart in places and doesn't always show Betty and Rosa in the best light. But then you aren't meant to *enjoy* medicine. You just hope it makes you better.

◆ The Scattering ◆

I WAS GLAD OF SIMON's funeral. Not that he was dead, of course, I wasn't glad about that — though on reflection, I was rather. Simon's been dying for months, each month getting a little more skeletal until you wondered how he could still stand up. Well, towards the end, he couldn't. He was in a wheelchair when I last saw him. It was in the theatre bar after a performance of *One for the Road!* Alan Munford's new play — Alan being an old pal of Simon's — and he had to be brought up in the lift and then somehow helped out of his wheelchair and propped up in an ordinary chair. He wasn't going to be confined. I suppose that's what that was about although it seemed hardly worth the effort because he'd chosen a rather deep armchair so that at home-time it took three people to help him out of it.

I have to say that about the head and face he was looking more and more like a memento mori — gaunt, eyes sunk in their sockets, skin like paper. Simon was one of those who take a long time dying. I've known others. There seems to be no rhyme or reason about it. Why it's sudden and quick for some and long and slow for others. Anyway, it's uncomfortable to watch the long slow ones even when they're brave — as Simon was — possibly that makes it worse. For the rest of us I mean. I found myself thinking that public dying should be forbidden, though you could make an exception for Simon because even though he was 86 and looked like a cadaver, he was still astonishingly handsome. You could see the Simon he had been in his bones. A part of it was his clothes, of course. He was always a dresser, a cashmere and soft cords man; elegant, just on the edge of, but not tipping over into, effete. Perhaps his pipe added a saving macho touch.

Sitting in the crematorium chapel alongside Stella and Leonard I thought that the only thing I'd really liked about Simon — apart from the fact that he seemed to like me and always touched my arm affectionately when we met — was his handsomeness. Of course he had a voice that went with it. In my opinion it doesn't matter how handsome a man is if his voice is unpleasant. It doesn't work the other way though — or not for me — a man with a lovely voice can get away with being almost ugly.

Anyway, sitting there while various eulogies were read by those who had known Simon as a friend or worked with him in the theatre — Sean Fellowes, the director of Simon's last plays, Mike Jarrett, drama critic of *The Telegraph*, a grandson with slicked hair and a frog in his throat — I felt slightly guilty, fraudulent even, that my affection for Simon was based on such a superficial thing as his looks and, too, that I was so vulnerable to beauty (I've been avoiding the word, but yes, Simon was beautiful) that this won him a fixed place in my affections. I'm not even sure if 'affection' is the right term. I merely liked *looking* at Simon. There was no desire attached to it. No curiosity. If I should say to Simon *I'm very pleased to see you*, that summed it up. I felt more affection for him now that he was dead than I had when he was alive. Maybe not affection. Gratitude. Gratitude for dying when he did, just before Christmas so that the funeral had to wait until after, which I know is hard for the family but in my case was just what I wanted. If someone had asked me, round about December 29th, in that period between Christmas and New Year, *what would you like to do today* — the honest answer would have been *I'd like to go to a funeral*.

In part, a funeral seemed just the right antidote to Christmas and prelude to New Year. So much so that I can't think why someone hasn't made it part of winter's ritual, a proper solstice. New Year's Eve is all partying. There's really not enough mourning attached to it. Auld Lang Syne doesn't do it for me. Apart from the almost trivial fact that apparently I was in the mood for a funeral, there was something else. In recent months I've become aware of an inexplicable sadness that seemed to have taken root deep down in me like the solid, muddy deposit in the very depths of the pond. Unlodgeable sorrow. I was not unhappy. Mostly I was cheerful, contented even, but all these genuinely good feelings lay on top of the sorrow. As though sorrow/sadness was the true core, as perhaps it is.

It was very peaceful at the crematorium. Had Simon asked for this particular one I wondered? Very likely. Built by a famous architect, it was shaped like a squeeze box, folds of stone with tall glazed slits for windows and set in parkland with a river running along one side. Non-denominational, it was discreet in its symbols, rather proudly allowing for funerals of Christians, Buddhist, Hindu, San, Sikh and Tao. There was even a 'Scattering Point' on the river for Sikhs and Taos. Inside was dark and calm with long pine pews and a platform of white concrete and bronze where the coffin rested. Simon wasn't anything, though one of his eulogists referred to a Jewish great grandfather who'd travelled from Lithuania and how Simon, this friend felt, would have wished to acknowledge this. It was the only faith not mentioned by the crematorium.

There were no prayers and no singing but I didn't mind. It had come upon me suddenly, the realisation that I wasn't there for Simon. I was there for my dead lover, Mark and my dead mother-in-law Jessica. I was at Simon's funeral because I hadn't been at theirs. And not being at theirs had left me feeling what? Uncomfortable. As if I was still carrying them around with me.

Why hadn't I gone to Mark's funeral? It would have been a Quaker one. Various friends, members of the family, would have spoken. Said nice things. Said loving things. I could have spoken. I could have said how his imagination had always half amused, half enchanted me. Enchanted. Yes. I'd been enchanted. What would have been the upset in that? The fear of upsetting had kept me away. I'd not wanted to upset Mark's daughters who knew of my existence, or his wife who with more than generosity tolerated me and my place in Mark's affections. At least this was the reason I gave myself, though in retrospect I became aware — was it the obituary notice that spoke of his wife as *his beloved Eileen* — of a certain belated and useless jealousy. At least I'd managed, on the day of his funeral, to go off to a quiet place among the tall, dark pines in the Botanic Gardens, to think about him, about the rebel qualities that got him sacked from the Central Electricity Generating Board for not keeping quiet about their use of plutonium, about the harpsichord he made and played, about being with him in Amsterdam and years later in Nigeria at the University of Kano. About him dying young. Sitting among the dark pines, mourning Mark, was the sadness growing then? A sadness not to do with Mark, hardly to do with me. I've heard it said they we carry our own death within us, as though we grow it. Lately, I've felt its weight somewhere that I think might be my solar plexus. Not soon, I say to myself, but one day. I'm a lady in waiting.

I could re-mourn Mark sitting there in the Crematorium. But Jessica? I became aware of just how much Jessica had been on my conscience about halfway through the service for Simon. A rather nervous and clearly amateur violinist was struggling through a Bach suite when it occurred to me that possibly I was using Simon as a kind of surrogate for Jessica.

Perhaps it was the knowledge of the Scattering Point on the river that prompted me to remember Jessica's ashes being taken home to Scotland as she'd always wished. I'd badly wanted to be there and 'badly' is perhaps the right word in several ways. *Badly* because I knew my being there would have angered Angus, my ex, and *badly* because I was enjoying a pleasant fantasy about turning up at the cemetery where Jessica was to be scattered among her ancestors, as the mysterious Other Woman, silent but of course darkly beautiful. (A hat or some head covering seemed very important to this fantasy). Did I love Jessica? Did I want to be there because I loved her? Not exactly. Fond. Yes. And admiring, although my admiration was for her glamour (cf Simon), her lovers, her independence and her dedication to her profession as a physiotherapist. She'd been the first independent, working woman I'd ever known.

Angus hated her. Never forgave her for abandoning him to the grandparents and a housekeeper while she was off trying to earn a living and, as a divorced woman, perhaps seeking a new man. She was, it must be admitted, incredibly manipulative and/or charming, depending on your response, but if the former, how long can a son remain unforgiving of his mother? Unto death it would seem. And as Angus was also unforgiving of me, Jessica and I had this unforgivingness in common. Long after my own divorce, Jessica and I stayed friends so that I was prone to joke that you can divorce a man but not a mother-in-law.

According to my daughter, the continued relationship, (full of Angus gossip and shared complaint), was 'inappropriate'. *Inappropriate* is a key word in Debbie's vocabulary. A counselling word, I suspect. Instead of an action or deed being good, bad or indifferent, loving, cruel or unkind, the moral judgement rested on the deed's appropriateness.

Anyway, I thought it was just Debbie's youth that made her think a continued relationship with an ex mother-in-law known for sixteen years, was inappropriate. Nevertheless, it was for Debbie's sake that I decided not to go to witness the scattering of Jessica's ashes. Debbie has suffered enough of the tug of love between mother and father. Her loyalties would be horribly torn if we were both there. So I'd told Jessica's daughter (another continued relationship) that on the day of the scattering I'd go to the Catholic Cathedral and light a candle for her mother. For Jessica. The Catholic Cathedral because — and again to Angus's annoyance — without exactly turning Catholic, Jessica was drawn that way. Had a knack of befriending nuns.

It was pouring with rain and blowing a gale on the day of the Scattering. The Catholic Cathedral turned out to be much further away than I'd thought. Something else cropped up. I couldn't be bothered. What was one candle, etc etc? Reason after poor reason. Though I did do it, several weeks later and in the Anglican Cathedral (decaff Christianity as I recall Simon calling it) but it didn't feel quite right. Out of sync. Not part of the ritual. It felt as if I'd failed her.

The violinist finished playing Bach. I observed a woman at the front — daughter, sister, mistress? — wiping her eyes. It is always better for everyone if someone cries. Observing her made me think that considering oneself, querying love and/or worrying about upsetting others, was entirely beside the point. When it comes to funerals, the question to ask oneself wasn't to do with love or upset or inappropriateness, it was *does this person — did Mark, did Jessica — want me to be there?* And the answer in both cases was yes. Mark because he loved me, had wanted me in his life. And Jessica? It came to me that Jessica would have liked me to be at the Scattering out of pure mischief; to upset folk (particularly Angus) and to create a little drama. Bagpipes, me and a little drama. That's what Jessica would have liked.

Before Simon was whooshed away, we were all asked to lay a flower on his rather fine wooden coffin. There was a basket full of chrysanthemum heads. I chose two white ones. I thought it was nice to send him off looking good. And after all, apart from his looks, Simon was a wise and understanding man. I thought he'd be glad I was there and that I'd come with my sorrow.

◆ The Noisiness of Sheep ◆

HARRY SAYS IT'S HIM or Agnes. He says I've got to choose. He says it's one thing being followed to school by a snowy little lamb when you're seven and quite another being stalked by a fat grubby ewe when you're seventeen. Harry says he doesn't want to be seen out with me. Me and Agnes that is. Harry says he's become a laughing stock.

I love Harry. I've loved Harry since I was fourteen. It's taken me three years of patient adoration to win him. Well, more than adoration really. Winning Harry has been like a campaign. I had to date Garth Lewis for three months to make Harry jealous. In fact I had to do a fair bit of stalking myself really. Just appearing, by chance as it were, at the tennis courts when Harry was playing a match. He's got a serve to make you melt. And he looks wonderful in his tennis whites. Well, he looks wonderful most of the time really.

Once upon a time — before we were an item — Harry thought Agnes was amusing. Everyone did. It's because of Agnes that people call me Mary. My real name's Stephanie but I hardly bother with that now. I've been Mary ever since my Dad bought me my first lamb as a birthday present when I was seven.

Actually I wanted a dog but my Dad had a thing about little girls and lambs. And that first lamb was terribly sweet. When I look in our old photo albums I can see that we made the perfect couple. Me with my hair in bunches and with blue ribbons and the lamb with a matching blue ribbon round its neck. The photo's taken in the back garden. The pair of us 'gambolling' — I think that's what lambs are meant to do isn't it? Anyway, we're the picture of innocence! We could have been in the garden of Eden that lamb and I. I reared it myself with a baby's bottle (there's another photo of that) and washed it under the shower to keep it snowy white.

But no it didn't follow me to school. Not that lamb and not the next one because my Dad bought me a new lamb on every birthday. My Mum got awfully fed up with it. In fact it's a wonder she didn't do a Harry and say 'either that lamb goes or I do'. But she's very tolerant my Mum and apart from his lamb fetish my Dad's a really nice bloke. Normal. Whatever my friend Andrea says.

Andrea says that giving your daughter a lamb every year is psychological abuse and that having a lamb at your heels forces you to be sweet and that feminists have worked really hard to stop us being sweet and if she was me she'd send the next lamb to the butcher's. No-one could say Andrea is sweet.

Anyway, when I was about twelve my Mum said, 'Jim, you've got to let Mary grow up' — even my mother called me Mary by then, I mean I was *known* by that lamb just as Andrea was *known* by her long ginger plaits — 'she's too old for lambs,' my mother said, 'how about a horse?'

'He won't get you a horse,' Andrea said. 'Horses are sexy.'

And she was right. I got Agnes instead. And Agnes was different from all the previous lambs. I mean I'd been fond of the others, but one lamb seemed much like another. I didn't get attached to them. Not the way I am with Agnes.

How can I explain? Agnes was an intelligent lamb. Understanding even. When I was upset she'd come and nuzzle me. Once, when our smoke alarm went off, she actually pulled me out of bed with her teeth. She'd begun sleeping in my room by then. And yes, it *was* Agnes who followed me. Followed me everywhere. School. The shops. The swimming pool. The library.

We read a poem at school recently. It's about a nymph and her faun and how this faun was so kind and pure it was like 'lillies without' and 'roses within'. Well, I know Agnes is nothing like a faun and, as Andrea would be quick to tell you, my thighs are too fat for a nymph. But the point is that although Agnes's fleece isn't soft and snowy white any more, but rather rough and grey and although, I admit, she does get a bit smelly these days, *at heart*, she's like that faun.

Andrea just said 'oh get real!' when I compared Agnes to the faun. But then in my opinion Andrea's never loved anyone but herself whereas my problem is that I love Agnes *and* Harry. Anyway, just before my thirteenth birthday, roundabout the time one lamb-come-sheep was replaced by another, I told my Dad I didn't want another lamb. I wanted to keep Agnes.

I think by then my Dad had lost interest in lambs. He'd begun an Open University Foundation course, he was into paintings of the Madonna. The original one, I mean. Andrea says this is just as suspect as lambs. She's very cynical is Andrea. She thinks my dad must have a mistress somewhere. 'Someone really tarty,' Andrea says. I don't think he's got the time with all those OU essays. But I suppose there is the Summer School…

Anyway, Agnes didn't go off to market like the other lambs. Agnes stayed. I suppose I did begin to think about getting rid of her about the time I first clapped eyes on Harry. I was in the third form and he was in the fifth form and even though he had a bit of acne it didn't matter because he was so hunky and he had dark hair that fell over his eyes so that he had to flip it back. He was shy and hunky then. That was before he realised that half the girls in the school fancied him.

It was through Agnes that I learnt that you can weather being laughed at. I mean there was a time when wherever I went — wherever *we* went, Agnes and I — someone would be sure to shout *Mint Sauce! Mint Sauce!* after us. And Agnes would lower her head and drag her little hooves and I knew her feelings were hurt, even if she didn't understand the threat of mint sauce.

But after a while people got tired of shouting mint sauce. In fact friends at school got quite fond of Agnes. Particularly Garth Lewis. He used to bring her apple peel every morning. Also I made Agnes some really cute headgear, braids and stuff. Agnes and me — we were sort of eccentric and trendy.

But all that was before Harry and I began going out together. And then I discovered that you can weather being laughed at, but you can't weather being in love. Not if you have a sheep that is.

Of course I tried leaving Agnes at home when Harry and I went out. I shut her in the back garden when we went to see *The Silence of the Lambs* (I didn't think it was very nice of Harry to chose a film like that, but still, we did have the back row ...) Anyway, Agnes may be too old to gambol these days, but she can still jump. And jump she did. Over the garden wall. Goodness knows how she got into town. I've heard stories of people who swear they saw her on the bus — the 23 that goes from outside our house — but I don't believe it, I really don't. But there she was, waiting outside the ABC for us and Harry was furious. Furious at having to walk through town with Agnes stomping behind us and some of his mates shouting really rude things at him. Things I can't repeat.

It wouldn't have been so bad if Agnes hadn't kept on BA-ing. BAA BAA BAA all the way home. I mean Agnes doesn't BA much. Maybe when my alarm clock goes off in the morning. Or sometimes if she hears a cat or an owl at night. So I knew all that BA-ing was a kind of protest. I knew she didn't like Harry.

After that night I tried to make sure Agnes stayed at home whenever I went out with him. But it wasn't easy. Agnes pined. She grew thinner and thinner and her fleece looked all manky. I could be wrong but I think she was just that little bit more smelly.

The really difficult times were when Mum and Dad went out and Harry and I had the house to ourselves. We'd snuggle up on the sofa with the telly and have a bit of a snog and well, it might have been a lot more than that if it wasn't for Agnes. If I shut her out of the room she just battered and butted at the door and went in for a long continuous BAAAAA BAAAA. I hadn't really thought about it before, but there's something terribly monotonous about a sheep's BAA. It can really get to you. It certainly got to Harry.

But then if I let her *in* the room, that was even worse. Agnes just stared at us. You know that glassy stare a sheep has? Agnes just stood there, four square and staring. That was when Harry totally lost his rag and said I had to choose. It was him or Agnes.

It wasn't an easy decision, I can tell you. I mean I *wanted* Harry, really wanted him. And the way things were going I thought it was going to be as hard to lose my virginity as it was to lose Agnes. I know it's awful of me, because Agnes has been such a dear, good friend — but I began to wish she'd die. Just naturally. That I'd wake up one morning and she'd just be — well, rug. After all, she's getting on a bit. But then so am I. I'll be eighteen next month.

Eventually I spoke to Dad. Of course I didn't tell him about Harry or my virginity beginning to weigh on me like a bad conscience. I just said I thought Agnes was getting old and maybe a bit arthritic, didn't he think? And I wouldn't want her to suffer. And next year I'd be going to college and obviously I couldn't take Agnes with me then, could I? How would he and Mum feel about looking after her while I was away?

D'you know, I don't think Dad's really looked at me or Agnes for at least a year. His vision must be clouded with Madonnas-and-Child, because when he looked at me he said, 'How long have you been wearing your hair like that?' And when he looked at Agnes he sort of recoiled. You'd think he'd have noticed the bits of fleece on the sofa or the droppings in the garden, but no, he's a one obsession at a time man, my Dad and lambs turning into sheep and little girls into big girls wasn't on his OU syllabus.

Mum said that maybe there was a kind of sheep sanctuary, like they have for donkeys, but we couldn't find one. So in the end it was a trip to the vet's for Agnes and me. And it *was* painless, I'm sure, even if Agnes did stare at me for what seemed an awfully long time and gave a kind of bleat, just as she had when she was a little lamb. So I cried. Quite a lot really. At least a box of tissues.

So that left me free for Harry. And the next night when my parents were out, Harry was round at our place p.d.q. Only it was odd. Suddenly I didn't fancy him any more. And it wasn't just that he didn't say a word about Agnes when everyone at school has been really sympathetic and Andrea even sent me a card saying 'sorry for your loss' — no, it wasn't just that. It was more that I didn't think him handsome and sexy any more. I thought his eyes were cold and his mouth had a cruel twist. And all that flicking back of his hair — a real poseur. The person Harry loves, I thought, is Harry.

Things never do turn out as you expect, do they? So now I've lost Agnes and kept my virginity. Still, I thought I might go back to Garth Lewis. Garth calls me Stephanie, not Mary. And I haven't forgotten the apple peel he gave to Agnes.

ACKNOWLEDGEMENTS

The following stories have been published
and/or broadcast:

'Trio' in T*he Bridport Prize Anthology*; 'The Novel
Novel Paper' by *Nonsuch*, University of Bristol;
'Just Breathing' in *Sex, Drugs, Rock'n'Roll* (Serpent's Tail);
'The Proposal', 'The Lady of the Sea', 'Female Company',
'The Noisiness of Sheep', 'Somebody Smith' and
'After the Snow Queen' BBC Radio 4; 'Mrs. McCoy
and Moses' in *God: an Anthology of Fiction* (Serpent's Tail);
'My Father as an Ant' in *Shorts: The Macallan
Scotland on Sunday Short Story Collection* (Polygon).
'The Sweet Possessive' by Radio Scotland;
'Somebody Palmer' (*Gutter*); 'The Scattering' (*Gutter*).

My thanks to my partner, Hamish Whyte
for patiently reading and re-reading these stories,
Sara Davies for broadcasting a number of them
on BBC Radio 4, my daughter, Kate Hendry
and my good chum Sarah Lefanu for
criticism and encouragement.